Through the Reflection

Abbie Price

ISBN:-10: 0-9972506-0-7
ISBN-13: 978-0-9972506-0-2

CONTENTS

CHAPTER I
ERIN

I sat on the edge of the pier and watched city lights appear in the darkness. I'd spent most of my life on Alcatraz Island, but I still felt the need to come here every night. The pier was where I felt relaxed. I dangled my feet over the edge, and the water below tickled the bottom of my feet. So far tonight was as normal as any other, but things were about to change very soon.

It was the last day of summer, and my older sister Annie and I had come up with the perfect way to celebrate. At night, we were going to paint all the leaves on the island reds, yellows, and oranges.

The leaves used to change on their own before the war, or at least that's what everyone says. But during the war, a strain of biological warfare managed to escape from a lab in San Diego. The virus didn't affect people, but it latched on to plants and tore their color changing ability away from them by altering their DNA. I've always wanted to know what the leaves used to look like in fall, so I decided: if nature can't change their color, I will.

I had been plotting this plan since summer began, and tonight my hard work was going to pay off. It had taken forever to gather supplies, create the plan, and convince Annie to help me. Now, I was finally ready. My plan was flawless, and nothing was going to stop me.

My dad worked as a prison guard, and he was in charge of the graveyard shift. He was nearly silent when he came home every night, but one thing always gave him away. The front door creaked as he opened it, and Annie and I could hear it from our room.

He would peek into our rooms out of habit, so we would have to wait a little longer before starting our plan. Once he was gone, we could sneak out the window; but the next part of the plan was trickier. We had to run to an abandoned shed behind our house without being noticed.

Avoiding all of the doors and windows would be difficult, but we couldn't do anything about it. For the past three weeks, Annie and I had been crushing berries to use as paint. We stored the paint in old flower pots inside the shed. This was the only place where they wouldn't be discovered.

After collecting our paint supplies, we were going to set up stations around the island. Each station would have one paint color and group of surrounding trees to paint. Our supplies were limited, so we couldn't mess up. I would have made extras, but the shed was already filled to the brim, and we had no other place to hide a surplus. This mission was strictly anonymous. No one could ever know it was us.

Once the stations were set up, we would start painting the leaves. We tied old rags to tree branches to use as paintbrushes. This way, we could easily destroy them afterwards.

Lastly, we would paint all the leaves; and we needed to be as fast as possible if we wanted to get home before the sun came up.

In the morning, all of the trees were going to be brilliant shades of red, orange, and yellow. It was the perfect way to celebrate the beginning of fall.

I watched as the city plunged into darkness, and I counted how long it took for the lights to appear. Usually, it took two or three minutes. When the lights appeared, I had only counted to one minute and twenty-seven seconds.

I wondered what caused them to turn the lights on so early. My mind was scanning itself for a possible explanation, and a million ideas formed. There were too many for me to consider, so I decided to enjoy the view for now and think about it later.

I had always wanted to know what it would be like to live in the city. I had only been there a few times for special occasions and it had been years since I last visited. Most of the other children went to the city every week. They attended schools on the edges of the city, but my mother homeschooled my sister and me. She didn't believe city schools provided a proper education.

I daydreamt about visiting the city every day. I

wondered if it was as beautiful as I remembered or if my memories were nothing more than a dream. I thought about asking one of the kids who goes to school there; but as soon as I got up, I heard the nine o'clock bell ring. This meant all of the kids who were still outside had to return home. I ran back to my house. I had ten minutes to get home after the bell, and the pier is at least a half mile from my home.

I could feel my long strides pushing me towards my destination. Whenever I ran, I felt like I was soaring through the air and above the clouds. It was one of my favorite things to do, and that was a good thing because that night, Annie and I had to run from station to station. If we didn't, we wouldn't get all the leaves painted or return home in time.

Once I reached the front porch, I stopped to catch my breath before letting myself in. I didn't want my mother to ask me where I had been. Last year, Alcatraz was turned into a secret underground prison. After that, my parents started to become insanely strict and overprotective.

Alcatraz had been retired for hundreds of years, but now it was needed once again for high security prisoners. The government couldn't come up with the money to build a new prison, so they had to use one that already existed.

Many people had previously been living here because the land was cheap, and it was the only place people could afford to live. When the transformation occurred, most of the families moved away. The few families who stayed were given jobs working at the prison. The parents put restrictions on our freedom and forced us to stay within a "safe distance from home."

I knew my parents would freak if they discovered I went to the pier every night, so I had to keep my trips there a secret. I had always been the more secretive child in my family.

Everybody knew me as Erin. And more importantly they all knew that I was very good at breaking the rules and not getting caught. Therefore, I loved creating complicated, exciting, rule-breaking plans — I especially loved being able to test them and see if they would work.

In my room, I had an entire binder filled with my ideas. Usually, I kept it hidden in my closet or under the bed. I could never risk being caught by my parents for my past schemes or have them prevent me from following through with any of my new ones.

I used to take pride in being different from everybody else, and most of the time I kept to myself. My sister always complained about not having my creativity and determination, but I would have traded anything to have her confidence. She always seemed to be certain about things, and there was never a time when she didn't know what she wanted or how to speak her mind.

I usually just went along with what everybody else said, and when I did have an opinion I never know how to express it. My thoughts were usually complex so I had trouble forming them into words.

However, I was very daring and I was willing to try almost anything. While other people had an endless number of fears, I only had one. I was afraid of letting my life go by and missing out on opportunities; so whenever I saw an opportunity, I took it.

Some people called this a weakness because I was willing to drop everything and do crazy things. People said I didn't have my priorities straight and I didn't set enough goals for myself, but they were wrong. My goal in life was to do as many things as possible. At the end of my life, I didn't want to have any regrets.

My hair was such a dark brown that most people thought it was black. It reflected sunlight, and I swear it could have blinded someone if I had lived somewhere sunny. My mother used to tell me I looked exotic, but most people on the island thought I was simply mysterious.

I was not sure if that was a good thing or a bad one, but I guess it could have been either. I had a sharp, distinctive jaw line and a pointed chin. My cheekbones were high, my lips were full, and my nose was a narrow ski-slope.

However, my favorite part about my face was my eyes. Unlike most people, my eyes were round and they showed no emotion. They were an amber-bronze color, and I was not sure what other people thought; but whenever I looked into my eyes, I felt like they were keeping secrets from me.

Sometimes I thought my mind was playing tricks on me, but other times I wondered if people thought I was keeping secrets from them. No one could ever know the real me when I looked them in the eye, they could only see two dark windows staring back at them.

In my opinion, my eyes made me look mysterious. And when I focused on them for a long time, I felt like a stranger to myself. I was slightly shorter than average, and

I had long legs and a short torso. I was sixteen years old.

Annie, my older sister, was eighteen. Unlike me, she had soft, delicate features. Although she was not as unusual looking as me, she was flawless. Her hair was long, wavy, and a rich brown color.

Her eyes were copper-colored, and they looked like pure honesty. Looking into them, you would think she'd never told a lie. Overall, her beauty was simple; but she was electrifying to anyone who laid eyes on her.

It scared the life out of me when Annie came up behind me and whispered in my ear: "I can't wait to paint the leaves tonight."

I almost jumped as I turned around to face her. I had been daydreaming again, but I couldn't tell her she scared me. If I did, she'd ask me what I was daydreaming about — and if I told her I was thinking about the city lights I would have gotten in lots of trouble. I responded by nodding my head in agreement, and we walked inside together.

When I walked inside, my mom was reading by the fire. There were two books sitting next to her, one for me and one for Annie. As part of homeschooling, the three of us read together every night. My mother chose the books we read; and while we were reading, we had to answer a list of questions she had written in the back of the book.

We usually read short chapter books, and occasionally our mother would read us a short story. After she finished telling the story, we had to discuss it and answer a list of questions. I silently picked up the book with my name on it and curled up on the couch with a soft, knit blanket.

We lived in a modest house. There was a family room for eating and socializing. And because we didn't have a guest room it doubled as a room for family members to stay when they came to visit us.

The room was small, but cozy. It had light brown walls with peeling paint, and dark green furniture with tears at the seams lined every wall. There was a small fireplace in the corner. It was made of chipped, cream-colored, clay bricks and the glass covering was stained gray with smoke.

The bedroom Annie and I shared was next door. It had two white twin beds with black comforters, two old white dressers, and a small overflowing closet. I kept everything I cared about in boxes under my bed because when something went into the closet, there was a good chance you would never see it again.

The only important thing I kept in the closet was my binder. A while ago I discovered a hidden compartment, and afterwards it became my hiding spot for my binder for awhile. However, I didn't know if Annie knew about it, so I ended up moving it back under my bed. I knew nobody would ever discover it there.

After I finished my story, I sat on the couch and daydreamed about the city lights again. I also thought about how much fun painting the leaves was going to be. I listened to the fire crackling, and I heard my mother and sister breathing in a slow, synchronized rhythm.

After a while, I heard my mother get up. She collected our work and books, and she walked to her room without saying a word. My sister and I walked to our room and lied down. We pretended to be asleep because we knew our mom would come in and make sure we were asleep any minute.

Afterwards, she would go back into her room. I'm not quite sure what she did in there. I never asked, and I never had a reason to find out. I convinced myself it wasn't important, and I began to go over our plan one more time. If I was forgetting about something, this was the time to remember it.

After going through the plan over and over again, I nearly fell asleep but then I heard the front door creak open. I listened as my father hung his jacket on the back of the door and set his shoes in the corner.

I waited until I couldn't hear anything but the sound of my heartbeat and the noises in my head. The things I hear at night have always confused me because I don't know if they're real or not. I know they're probably coming from the prison or our neighbors (the walls in our house are thin enough that you could hear a pin drop in the other room), but I can't help wondering if this logic is wrong. I feel like the noises are coming from the ground, and no matter how many times I push away the feeling, it always ends up coming back.

Anyway, I rolled out of bed and clumsily made my way across the room to Annie. I shook her awake and she started to moan.

"I don't want to get up; can't you just do it without me?" she groaned.

I told her, "No, Annie, you promised you would do this so you are going to follow through with it."

I walked over to the window and slid it open. The last time I had opened it had to have been years ago because it was nearly rusted shut. I slid the window and hoped I hadn't made too much noise in the process. Annie was just getting out of bed, and I watched her stumble towards me.

I swung my right leg over the windowsill and climbed out of the window. There were a few times when I started to panic because I couldn't remember how far down the drop was. I didn't feel safe until I had both of my feet firmly planted on the ground again.

Annie reached under her bed to get our winter coats, and tossed them out the window to me. She hesitated when it came to climbing out of the window; so as soon as both of her feet were dangling from the window, I took hold of them and pulled her onto the ground.

By this time, both of us were already panting like dogs. We crawled to the shed where our paint was hidden. We couldn't stand up because if we did, we could be seen through the windows. I was not going to get caught before we had even started our work.

We were covered in dirt by the time we reached the shed, but I didn't care. Adrenaline was pulsing through my veins. We were one step closer to being successful. I cautiously slid the shed door, and we shuffled into the shed. I'm sure we looked like zombies walking around. We had our hands out in front of us, and we were shuffling our feet so we wouldn't run into anything.

The shed door swung closed behind us, and my foot bumped into a flower pot filled with paint. I lifted the pot and kicked the shed door open with my foot. I could feel my arm muscles bulging; and when I handed the pot to Annie, my arms felt limp. She placed the pot in front of the door to prop it open, and I started to pick up the next pot.

This process continued until all twelve buckets were sitting outside of the shed. I wished we could paint the shed with the leftover paints, but we would definitely get caught if we tried to do that.

We evenly dispersed the buckets around the island according to color. In the end, there would be a red section of trees, then a section of orange, and lastly yellow. This pattern repeated four times, and when every station had a bucket of paint and a brush, we began to paint.

Annie started on the far side of the island, and she planned to work her way back to the house. I started near our house, and I planned to work my way over to the far side of the island.

Once the sun began to rise, I knew I would have to sprint across the island. It was the only way I could get home in time. I would have liked to work in the same direction as Annie; but starting at opposite ends would be easier and make us more efficient.

The longer I painted the leaves, the more peaceful it became. I could hear waves crashing up on the shore, and the wind was whistling as it blew through the trees. Soon, I didn't even have to think about painting the leaves anymore. It felt like I had done this a million times.

The first few leaves were difficult because I couldn't figure out how much paint to put on them. Some of them had hardly any paint, and some of them started drooping from the weight of the paint.

When I finally discovered the right amount of paint to use, I started to imagine I was Picasso in his blue stage, Leonardo Da Vinci painting the *Mona Lisa*, and Van Gough painting *Starry Night*.

I'd never had so much fun in my life, and I was already plotting plans to do this sort of thing for every season. However, the most magical thing was looking up and watching the stars glittering in the sky. I'd heard kids talking about sneaking out to see the stars before, and they always said it was magical. I had never quite believed them, but I did now.

They weren't only magical, they filled you with hope. I was eager to spend more time admiring the stars, so I hurried through the rest of my stations. I never thought something so far away could be so motivating.

I worked faster than I ever had before; and when I finished, I had plenty of time to spare. I walked part of the way. This way, I wouldn't have to worry as much about making my way home. I lied down on a hill and cleared my mind of everything but stars.

I probably went minutes at a time without blinking. I didn't want to waste a single second of this moment. I drew imaginary lines that connected the stars and formed shapes. When I finally became bored, I started to think of silly stories to go along with the pictures I made.

My favorite story I made up was called Hunter the Hunter. It was about a hunter named Hunter who traveled the land looking for something to eat. However, he was very stupid and made all of his arrows out of paper.

Whenever he hit an animal with one of his arrows

the animal would run away or attack him. One day, Hunter was attacked by a moose and afterwards, he met a beautiful huntress named Huntress. Huntress taught Hunter how to make arrows out of wood, set snares, and catch animals by surprise.

They spent days hunting with each other, but eventually Huntress had to return to her tribe. Hunter tried to come with her, but he was immediately banished. That night, he watched in silence as Huntress and her tribe celebrated her return.

The group left early the next morning, but Hunter didn't know because he was still sleeping. When he found out they had left, he made himself a promise: he would do whatever it took to find Huntress and become a member of their tribe. He never stopped searching for Huntress, and he never stopped believing that he will find her.

I couldn't stop thinking about what I would have done if I was in Hunter's place. After a while, I decided that I would do the same thing as he did. I would keep going and never give up or lose faith.

For the first time in a while, I felt truly happy. Then, I heard a loud shriek in the distance. I knew Annie was in trouble, and my spirits instantly sank. I sprang into action, and I began running toward Annie.

I charged down the hill and took a sharp left turn, but I was unaware of the rock wall in front of me. I smacked into it at full speed and every breath in my lungs flew away from me. I was left gasping for air.

I fanned air into my mouth, but my lungs kept rejecting it. I'm sure it was only a few moments before I started breathing again, but it felt like a lifetime. I knew I had a gash on my scalp because I was blind from blood. I could taste it when I breathed through my mouth, and my hair was a sticky, wet, disgusting mess. I felt paralyzed from the impact, and my ears were ringing. I couldn't hear anything around me.

But even through all the pain, all I could think about was Annie. I hoped she hadn't been caught by a guard or taken by a runaway prisoner. I knew that if anything happened to her, it would be my fault. The guilt would be imbedded in me forever like a scar.

As I sat up, my bones slid back into place and I could hear a million tiny cracks. I had to sit for a moment while I tried to control my breathing and create a game plan to save Annie. This was the hardest plan I had ever made because I had no idea what the situation was.

For all I knew, she could be anywhere and with anyone. I ignored the pain and rose to my feet. Instantly, I collapsed to my knees. I wiped the blood away from my eyes and slid my palms along my pants to dry them.

I crawled until I reached the wall, and I lifted my hand to the nearest rock. I used the wall to steady myself as I stood up; but I never fully regained my balance, so I had to lean against it as I walked.

I was shaking and I could feel my hands sweating. At last, I reached the end of the wall. Standing before me was a giant tree. I couldn't tell what kind it was because blood was filling my eyes again. I knew I had to move fast. I was losing a lot of blood.

I spotted a branch nearby on the ground, so I

stretched my leg out as far as I could to get it. I could just barely reach the end, but I was still able to drag it towards me. When I bent over to get it, I felt like my bones were being torn apart.

The pain was worse than anything I had ever felt before. I closed my eyes and held my hand over my mouth to keep myself from screaming out in pain. For the first time, I realized I was crying.

Crying wasn't a normal thing for me because when I took risks, I was smart and I stayed away from things that could hurt me. The only other times I could remember crying were at funerals, but those tears weren't real. The tears only came because I had seen them on everyone else's faces. At the time, crying was a form of camouflage for me.

I felt a sense of relief flow through me when my hand clasped the branch. I gripped it as tightly as I could. I'm sure it made my hands and forearms turn white. Standing up was much easier then bending over, but I knew my muscles and bones were still shifting. Now and then, I heard a loud pop, snap, or crack.

Luckily, the sound was much worse than the pain that came with it. I leaned my weight onto the branch, and I slowly released the wall. Using the branch for support, I limped toward where I heard the shriek coming from. I'm sure I'm not the only one who heard it, and I most likely wasn't the only one searching for its owner. I just hoped I could get to Annie before anything bad happened.

Several times I thought about giving up and going home. I had lost a lot of blood, and I was badly injured. It would have been the smartest choice to make, but I knew it wasn't an option. My face was caked with blood and I could barely see anything, but I kept moving forward.

I finally reached one of the stations. I was positive that Annie was here when she screamed. I called out her name a little louder every time I said it. It felt like I should be screaming, but my voice was no louder than a croak.

I turned around to start heading in a different direction, but then I saw a bucket of paint. It was red, but in the moonlight it looked like blood. The sight of it made me feel queasy, and I shuddered a little bit. The bucket had been pushed onto its side, and all the paint had spilled out of it and formed a small pool of liquid.

Annie wouldn't have knocked it over, and she wouldn't have screamed if she saw a guard. This meant she must have heard a criminal escaping. When she heard them, she would have tipped the bucket. They would have heard the noise and ran away because they thought prison guards were around. She would have ran after tipping the bucket, but judging from her scream; they spotted her, and they knew she wasn't a guard.

It wouldn't have been a prisoner who knocked over the paint. If you were smart enough to escape the prison, you wouldn't be stupid enough to run into a flower pot. If Annie had run fast enough, she would have made it home before she was caught. Then, the prisoners would be returned to their cells.

However, if she wasn't fast enough, they would have taken her. At this point, I didn't care what happened to me or how furious my over-protective parents were going to be. I had to get home and make sure Annie was alright. Getting in trouble was now the least of my worries.

I stumbled over uneven ground on my way home, and I would have fallen if I hadn't had the branch to catch myself; but when it caught me, it stabbed into my hand and left a deep cut. My palm instantly started gushing blood.

Within minutes, the entire branch was bloody and hard to keep a hold of. I nearly dropped it several times; and when it slipped out of my hand, it took me down with it. I thought about getting back up; but it was so dark, and my face was covered in blood. I couldn't see anything.

I started to wonder what I looked like. My clothes were ripped; and they were covered in dirt, dust, and mud. My face and hair were caked with blood and my hand was still gushing blood like a volcano.

If someone saw me now, I wondered if they would help me or leave me as I bled to death. I knew I had lost too much blood when I started to lose my peripheral vision. Soon after, everything else became a blur.

I felt something wrap around me. I thought that my imagination was playing tricks on me. It felt much too strong to be human; and instead of hands, it had claws connected by multiple layers of webbing.

I felt myself being pulled downward. The pain I felt was excruciating, and no part of my body was spared. Hot tears filled my eyes, and they began flowing out in a thick, even stream. They washed enough blood from my face that I could fully open my eyes, and I didn't taste blood in my mouth anymore.

I tried to stop my tears as soon as they started. I

didn't want to die crying; and the further I fell, the closer I came towards death. I hoped Annie was alright, and if she did face death, I hoped it wasn't as miserable as mine. Soon the downward feeling stopped, and I wondered if that meant I was dead.

Afterwards I felt a feeling like no other. It felt like I crashed into solid cement and shattered every bone in my body. I envisioned the millions of tiny pieces spraying across every square inch of the floor.

I wanted to scream out in pain, but couldn't. I had started coughing up blood. My vision soon returned, but it was only for a second. To this day, I wish that second had never happened. What I saw scarred me for life, and I will never forget it.

I was sitting in the middle of a pool of my own blood, and in front of me was the mutt- like creature that brought me here. I was correct, it had no hands. They had been replaced by razor-sharp claws with thick webbing between them.

I gingerly touched my arms and felt where they had pierced my flesh. They stung like powerful acid had been poured into them. The mutt's face was masked, and its eyes were blood red. They were the crazed eyes of a murderer. Its body was cloaked in black, and there was a single red dot placed where its heart should have been.

I fell unconscious in a matter of seconds. I remember dreaming about painting the leaves with Annie. I never knew things could change so much in one night. A few hours ago, I'd had a whole life ahead of me. Now, I was waiting to die.

I started whimpering, and soon after I heard a voice. "She's alive," it spoke softly, but I couldn't have heard the words more clearly.

CHAPTER II
ALEX

A long time ago, a vicious storm swarmed the earth. Very few people survived, and everything else was destroyed. The few survivors soon started to die from starvation, and eventually they became desperate. They turned to cannibalism, and they had no mercy for one another.

However, one group of people was spared. They belonged to an ancient tribe who worshipped higher beings. All of their legends turned out to be true, and these higher beings protected and provided for the tribe.

Then, the beings disappeared. No one ever saw them again, and the tribe was left to fend for themselves. No matter how desperate they became, the tribal people never turned on one another. Together, they sought a place to escape the greedy cannibals.

When they came across a mysterious island, they

decided to make it their new home. They spent many centuries creating an array of tunnels that led underground. Within these tunnels, a city was created and named Millennia. The tunnels interlocked and formed a maze to keep cannibals away.

In the end, the maze protected the city. Anyone who went through an entrance became lost in a series of tunnels. Within these tunnels, many deadly obstacles had been created. These obstacles could kill you if you made even a single mistake.

The people in the city had maps of the tunnels. Every map showed where obstacles were, and they had a set of directions telling you how to get past them alive. Every leap year, a man would be chosen to leave the city. He would go through the maze and bring back new information about the land above.

This happened for hundreds of years. There were many deaths and injuries, but a man finally came back untouched. He said the cannibals had died off, and it was safe to live on the surface again.

The city of Millennia feasted and celebrated as they packed all of their belongings. Only a handful of people in the city had ever seen sunlight before. The only light source in the city was torches. They lined most walls in the city, and everywhere else was covered in darkness.

Everyone was ready to return to the surface, but that night something terrible happened. A torch fell and lit the map room on fire. Without the maps, the people had no hope of returning to the surface.

Many people died in the fire trying to salvage maps.

Groups would venture into the maze and try to navigate it themselves, but they were never seen again. No one knows if they escaped or if they died trying.

Eventually, the people accepted that they were trapped. They would have to continue living in Millennia or face the malicious maze. There were rumors of cannibals in the maze. People believed anyone who entered would end up being eaten alive.

My sister, Ria died in the maze. I don't know how. All I know is one day she left, and she never came back.

People said they had seen her enter the maze, but no one followed her and no one waited for her come out. Since then, my brother, And and I have stayed as far away from the maze as possible. Ria and I were twins, and And is two years older than us. He's nineteen and I'm seventeen.

Most people who aren't from Millennia would say Alex, And, and Ria are strange names, but they are perfectly normal. In Millennia, everyone shares a name with their siblings, and each child goes by a portion of it. The name I share is Alexandria.

However, ever since Ria left us, people call us Alexand. I don't mind it, but Alexandria will always be my name. I know Ria's name was only taken out because my parents were extremely depressed after her disappearance. They didn't talk for days, and they never left the house.

To this day, they don't leave the house unless they absolutely have to. They avoid talking to people, and sometimes I go weeks without hearing their voices. The only exception to this was yesterday. This was when a mysterious girl arrived in Millennia.

And and I were taking a walk together when we found her bleeding to death. It was near the graveyard. We had been on our way to visit our sister's tomb.

We patched the girl's wounds as best as we could, but it was hard to tell where they started and ended. I stitched the gash on her scalp with a paperclip and dental floss. Afterwards, she wasn't bleeding as much, so And and I carried her home.

When we arrived at the door, our mother was horrified. She and my father immediately started tending the girl's wounds as if she was their own child.

I hadn't seen my parents act like this since before we lost Ria. They were talking to us and asking us to tell them everything we knew about the girl. There wasn't much to tell, but we told them how we found her and brought her here. They listened carefully as they tended her wounds. As time went by, it felt like our family was becoming more of a family again.

I know it sounds crazy that a perfect stranger could just waltz into our lives and completely change everything, but there was something different about her. My trust has never been an easy thing to earn, but she gained it the moment I saw her.

When I was around her, I felt calm and in control. It was as if nothing bad could ever happen when she was around. She made me feel powerful and important just through her presence.

My family never said anything about the way she made them feel, but they didn't have to. I knew they felt the same way. Her presence put us all at ease, and she made it possible for us to escape all of our worries and misery.

But the craziest thing was: I could feel the effect she had on me before she had even opened her eyes. However, she wasn't the only one who had this mysterious power. I felt the same way when I was around And, and I had felt the same way around Ria as well.

When I realized the girl was waking up, I immediately announced it, and my family came rushing over. We stood over her as she opened her eyes and looked around in confusion.

I told her, "Everything's okay. My name is Alex. This is my brother And, and these are my parents." I explained to her how we'd found her bleeding to death, and how we tended to her wounds.

I even admitted to her that we'd started to have doubts whether or not she would survive. She had been with us for nearly a month, and before this, a faint pulse was the only sign of life she had showed.

After a while she finally replied, "I thought I was dead."

I laughed and said, "You were pretty close, and you lost a lot of blood, but you'll be fine." I knew I shouldn't — but I couldn't help myself, so I asked, "Do you remember what happened?"

"My sister and I were painting the leaves as a celebration of fall," she began, "everything was going according to plan, but then I heard this scream. I knew Annie was in trouble. I tried to run to her, but I ran into a rock wall and got a gash all along my scalp. That's when I started to lose blood. I could barely walk, and I had to use a tree branch as a crutch. When I got to where I heard the scream coming from, Annie was nowhere to be found. I slipped and the branch pierced through my hand. After that, I couldn't get up. Something grabbed me from behind and pulled me under the surface. I only saw a glimpse of it before I went unconscious. It was cloaked in black with a matching mask. Above its heart was this red dot. It had claws with thick webbing between them, and its eyes were totally bloodthirsty."

When she finished, I was horrified. The cannibals were still alive, and they were living in the maze. All I could bring myself to say was, "I'm sorry about your sister. I lost a sister somewhat recently, and I know how terrible it is. I hope she's alright and doing well."

"Thank you, I hope the same thing is true for your sister," she responded.

"I'm sure you're hungry," my mother interrupted. "We have a little of everything, what would you like?"

"I'm not very hungry right now," the girl answered, "but thank you so much for being so nice to me. I hope I haven't caused any problems for you."

"Not at all!" my mother exclaimed, "It's been wonderful having you with us. Oh, and what's your name?"

"Erin," she choked. I could tell she was a bit uneasy about everything that was going on, and I hoped we hadn't said anything to upset her.

"Well, it's nice to meet you Erin," my mother spoke softly and her voice had a tinge of disappointment. I think she'd been hoping for the girl to be Ria, and I couldn't blame her. I'd been hoping for the same thing. After all, the two looked identical.

The next few days Erin didn't do much other than rest and regain her strength. And when she was finally ready to talk, the whole family was there.

However, she seemed overwhelmed with all of us there, so I said, "Do you want to go for a walk and get some fresh air? I'm sure it would feel nice to get out of this stuffy room." I couldn't tell what she was thinking. Her eyes were emotionless, but she nodded. I helped her up, and I could tell she was still in pain. She was squeezing her eyes shut and biting her lip.

We walked out of the house and down the street in silence. She still needed a crutch to walk, but every step she took seemed to be easier than the last. Finally, I broke the silence.

"How old are you?" I asked.

"Sixteen," she responded.

She raised her eyebrows to ask me the same question.

"Seventeen," I replied, "where are you from?"

"I live on this island called Alcatraz," she hesitated as if remembering something, and then she added, "It's above the surface and it has a super high security prison. My dad works as a prison guard, so our whole family lives on the island."

"That's amazing," I breathed, "I've never left Millennia before. What's it like on the surface?"

"It varies;" she spoke softly, "Alcatraz has almost no one living on it. It's about a mile away from a big city called San Francisco. Tons of people live there, and every day the streets are full of people wandering around. I love it in the city, and one day I hope I get the chance to live there."

"Cool," was all I could bring myself to say. I had always been intrigued by the surface. I hoped to find myself there one day.

"So what's it like in Millennia?" she asked.

"Boring," I laughed, "there's not really anything to do until you turn twenty. That's when you're selected for a job by the elders. You become an apprentice for someone, and when the time comes you take their place. And is only nineteen, so we go on walks every day together. Meanwhile, daring kids wander into the maze."

"What's the maze?" she questioned.

I told her the history of Millennia: how the maze was built as protection, how people were sent to collect information about the cannibals, and about the fire that destroyed every maze map in existence.

Lastly, I told her about Ria and how after that, everything changed. She listened carefully, and when I finished she stood in silence as if taking everything in.

"Wait, so I'm stuck here forever now? I'm never going to see my family again?" she blurted, "I don't care if the maze is dangerous and infested with cannibals or whatever. We are going to find a way out. We will rescue Annie and your sister and everything will be all good and normal again."

I was in such shock. All I could say was, "We have a deal." I knew it was a stupid decision, but I couldn't help myself from thinking she was right. We could save her sister, find Ria, and reach the surface. The idea filled me with hope and excitement.

"Good," she smiled, "we'll pack supplies this afternoon and leave at midnight. We can't tell anyone because judging from what you've said, they'll try to stop us. We can leave a note or something so they don't get too worried, but we have to make sure they know not to come after us."

I nodded. We had reached the edge of the city, and the maze was looming before us. I couldn't believe I was about to risk my life in the maze with a complete stranger, but I didn't have any other choice.

The effect she had on me was stronger than anyone could ever imagine, and I felt like a different person when I was around her. In that moment if someone had been able to read my thoughts, then they would have pegged me to be insane.

In my mind, the person I became around her was someone I was proud to be; and I refused to lose that person when I had only just found her.

I turned around and whispered, "We better head back before they start to worry about us, not to mention the fact that we have a lot of preparation to do."

We both smiled. Somehow, I knew we were going to survive the maze and accomplish what we set out to do. We walked home in silence, and I knew both of us were already forming plans in our heads.

When we got home, everyone was waiting for us. The table was set, and dinner was ready to eat. It surprised me because we hadn't had a family dinner for a long time. Everyone raided the pantry when they got hungry, but having a proper dinner felt as normal as breathing due to Erin's presence.

My mother was the first to speak up, "I hope you're hungry; we have enough food to feed a small army."

We all laughed and smiled. It had been a long time since my mother had made any jokes. It seemed like Erin had come into our lives at the perfect time. With her, our family was beginning to become a real family again.

The entire time we ate, Erin and I exchanged looks of excitement. I had mentally come up with a list of supplies we would need, but there was no way to start strategizing until we knew what we were up against.

After dinner, we all cleaned the kitchen and did the dishes together. Once the kitchen was clean, we went into the family room to play games together. We didn't have many games, so we spent most of our time playing Maze Travels. Maze Travels is a game where you have to make your way through a maze and back without being killed by another player.

Each person also has four obstacles they can use to stop or inconvenience someone else. When it is your turn, you can either place an obstacle or move five inches in any direction. If you end up in the same place as someone else, they die and are out of the game.

Erin was surprisingly good at the game for having never played before. This gave me a sense of relief. The person I was going into the maze with was clever and creative.

The entire time we played, everyone was laughing and getting to know each other. Erin mainly asked questions about Millennia and the maze. We mostly asked her questions about herself and life on the surface.

She told us about city lights that she watched appear from the darkness every night, and being homeschooled by her mother. Right now, life on the surface sounded better than ever.

Once everyone had gone to bed, Erin and I snuck back downstairs to collect supplies. We each had an old beat up backpack filled with food, medical supplies, and other useful stuff like knives and rope, but right before we walked out the door, And appeared from behind a column in the kitchen. Then, he started to question us about where we were going.

"Where are you going? It's one in the morning!" he whisper-shouted.

At that point, I had no choice but to tell him the truth. After I finished explaining, I begged, "Pllleeaasssseeee don't tell Mom and Dad. I don't want them to worry."

"On one condition," he replied.

"Anything," I promised.

"I want to come with you," he stated.

"But..," I began.

"No excuses," he interjected. "Either you let me come with you, or I will go tell Mom and Dad about your plan right now."

"Fine," I agreed.

"Good," he smirked, and after he finished packing

his own bag he asked, "Ready?"

"Ready as we'll ever be," Erin piped up.

When we got to the maze, there were three different paths: one to the right, one to the left, and one down the middle.

Erin was the first to speak up, "We should take lefts at every turn. Then, if we get lost and have to come out we won't get even more lost."

It was an excellent idea, and I knew she had been planning ahead. I silently prayed that her clever mind would be enough for us to survive and succeed. And agreed that it was a good plan, so we turned left into the maze.

CHAPTER III
ERIN

To most people, it would seem strange to go on a life and death mission with two strangers; but somehow, I felt like I'd known And and Alex my entire life.

In my head I rationalized my thoughts by convincing myself that they had saved my life and taken me in. Therefore, I didn't have to worry about them murdering me in my sleep or anything. After all, it wouldn't have made sense if they spent months bringing me back to life just to kill me.

Alex had short, coffee-brown hair with maple eyes. He was tall and strong with a rugged but comforting face. His nose was a steep slope sprinkled with freckles, and his perfect cheekbones made his smile irresistible. His personality shone through the light in his eyes. I could tell just by looking at him that he was courageous, shrewd, and daring.

And had honey-colored hair. It hung just above his eyes, and it brushed against his eyelashes when he widened his eyes. His eyes were ice blue and they never failed to hold your attention. His jaw line was sharp, but it softened out as it curved. He was lean but at the same time he was made out of pure muscle. His thin shirt revealed a perfect six pack, and his shoulders were broad and strong. He had to be over six feet tall, and he moved with confidence everywhere he went.

I hadn't talked to him much because he was very quiet compared to his brother, and he mainly kept to himself. I hoped I would learn more about him while I was here. If not, this was going to be a long, awkward journey.

For the first fifteen minutes or so, we all walked in silence. The maze was cold, and the walls were wet. The floor was slippery in the middle, so we all walked in a line along the left side of the tunnel. Again, I was the first one to break the silence.

"How many times have you guys been in here before?" I asked.

"None," Alex quickly answered.

"One," And shuttered.

"What are you talking about? You have never said anything about that before," Alex questioned.

"I knew you would want to go into the maze if you knew I had, and I didn't want to be a bad influence. I didn't think you would ever have to know," And whispered.

"Well, I'm here now," Alex glared at his brother, "and I think we all would like to know about your experience."

"I will tell you if you promise not to interrupt me. Save all of your comments and questions until I am done," he negotiated. Alex and I quickly nodded to confirm his offer.

"Good," he said, and he lowered his voice before continuing. "About a month or so before Ria disappeared, I met a girl named Kate. She was the oldest of Katelyn, and although she was insanely daring, she was irresistible. I couldn't say no to her. She persuaded me to sneak out and explore the maze with her."

"We were only a few turns into the maze when I tripped and fell. I sliced my hand open and stopped to bandage it. She hadn't noticed, and she took the next turn. As soon as she was out of sight, I heard a scream..," he paused.

"The cannibals are real. They have adapted to maze life and made the maze their home. That's why the maze is so dangerous. The obstacles usually don't kill people, they only slow them down. The cannibals are responsible for most disappearances in the maze. Very few people die from starvation or getting lost."

"When the screaming stopped and she didn't come back, I knew she was dead. I darted out of the maze; and when I was safe, I leaned against a city wall and started to cry."

"My blood soaked the gauze on my hand and started dripping onto the ground. I tried to understand what had happened, but it took me weeks to realize the cannibals were responsible for all of the disappearances."

"The night after I figured it out, we lost Ria. That's

why I never allowed you to go near the maze. I barely knew Kate, but her death combined with Ria's was too much for me to handle. If I lost you, there would be no reason for me to live anymore."

Alex and I stood with our eyes popping out of our heads and our mouths hanging open. A million questions rushed to my head, but I had to let Alex ask his questions first.

"Why have you been keeping so many things from me?" Alex questioned, "You never told me about Kate, you didn't tell me about your trip to maze, and you kept the cannibals a secret!"

"I wanted to," And looked down in despair, "but I didn't want you to get any ideas. I promised myself I would do whatever it took to keep you safe and away from the maze. As for the cannibals, I couldn't bring myself to talk about them because I didn't want to believe it. I wanted to believe Kate, Ria, and everyone else had lived and made it to the surface."

All Alex said in response was "Oh."

"Do you think we have a chance of, you know, surviving the maze?" I shuddered at the thought of what could happen, and I quickly pushed it out of my mind.

"Yes," And answered, "as long as we stay alert and don't do anything stupid, I believe we should be fine." I felt a sense of relief wash over me, but it quickly vanished when he added, "As for finding Ria and your sister, Annie, I am not sure if that's possible. All I know is that we are going to try, and hopefully we'll get lucky."

I nodded in response. I knew he was trying to be

positive, but I couldn't fully believe him. His voice shook when he spoke, and his eyes were uncertain.

I felt like he was keeping something important from us, but I didn't want to pressure him into saying something he didn't want to admit.

We stood in silence as we evaluated the situation. I knew turning back was the smart thing to do, and that part of me wanted to run out of the maze screaming like a little girl in a horror movie, but I couldn't be a coward.

I had nearly bled to death, and my sister had disappeared. I wasn't going to let a near stranger's story make me do something if it was against what I believed in. I believed in never being a coward and using my fears to my advantage. By learning from them and overcoming them, I knew I would be provided with strength and knowledge.

"If the two of you would like to continue on our little quest, I suggest we keep moving and find a safe place to set up camp for the night. We won't be able to make educated decisions if we are not rested, and if we keep standing around like this, we'll waste all of our energy," And stated. "However, if you don't want to continue, I suggest we get out of here and return home as soon as possible. That is if you don't want Mom and Dad to worry," he looked straight at Alex.

Alex and I turned to each other and nodded. We both were going to be strong and do what we had set out to do.

I looked at And and said, "Lead the way."

And walked swiftly and confidently, while Alex and

I walked clumsily behind him. We jumped every time someone stepped on a twig or leaf. And took every turn like he knew exactly where he was going and had no doubt about it. After about twenty minutes or so, we came to an abrupt stop. We had hit a dead end, but judging from And's expression, this is what he had wanted to happen.

He turned to us and said, "Time to set up camp." We all dropped our backpacks on the ground and sat while we sorted through them. Using the blankets and rope, we built a tent. We tied the ropes to the vines along the maze wall and draped blankets over them.

Building it reminded me of when Annie and I were younger and built forts in the living room together. When it was finished we all walked into our homemade tent and sat on a blanket that we had draped across the ground.

As I looked around I realized that all of the blankets were different. The ones we had at home were all identical navy blue with black seams. The one directly in front of me was a bright yellow with a picture of a rainbow that spread from one end to the other.

The second one was green and blue striped and the condition was terrible. It was unraveling at the edges and had lots of little tears and holes throughout the center. The next one was a vibrant orange with deep red polka dots. This one was worn as well; however, it was not as severe as the others.

The last one was the one we were sitting on. It was solid black apart from the small silver stars along the edges. It was soft, thick, and for the most part it was in perfect condition. The only hint that it had ever been used was a small blue stain in the corner.

I felt comfortable in the tent because it felt familiar. In a place that was so different from what I was used to, even the small things felt important.

I know it shouldn't have surprised me but it completely shocked me when And said, "All of us should carry a weapon. If we run into any cannibals we need to be able to defend ourselves. I suggest you attach it to one of your belt loops so you will have quick, easy access to it. I wasn't sure if you had grabbed anything to keep weapons in so I grabbed us each one of these." He held up a small pouch that was the perfect size for storing a knife or a small gun.

Alex and I each took a pouch from And and we reached for our bags. We dug through them until we found the knives we had packed. We each had one and they were identical.

It was about the size of my forearm, and had a rough, leather handle. The blade glistened as I tilted it back and forth to inspect it. It was spotless and had no signs of ever having been used.

I prayed that I would not be the first to use it. I lifted the pouch and slid the knife in. The leather on the pouch matched the handle of the knife, and there was a small leather loop hanging from the top. I used it to fasten the pouch to the belt loop on my pants.

And and Alex did the same, and when I looked at their knife holders, I realized that they were identical to mine. I wondered if the knives had come in a set or if it was just a coincidence that they were all the same.

And sensed my confusion and explained, "The knives are all the same as you have probably figured out. They are one of the only things left from the surface. When people first settled in Millennia they protected everything they had, but over the years we have been changing old things into new ones."

"Every family is only allowed to have one item from the surface, and they must surrender the rest to the government to be used for a new purpose, like new torches or coins. Anyway, Mom and Dad chose to keep this set of three knives because they planned to pass one on to each of us — meaning myself, Alex, and Ria — when we had grown up and moved from the house. They are also special because they have been passed down from generation to generation along with the stories of our people."

"I remember listening to my grandpapa tell stories for hours and hours when I was a little boy. My favorite one was about when he fought his way against the cannibals into the maze. He was surrounded by them and all he had to defend himself were these knives. He killed them one by one as they approached him. They were human, but they couldn't control themselves. As he sliced through them, they oozed a slimy, green liquid instead of blood. This was the only sign that they were different from humans — apart from their behavior."

"Some people think the cannibals became so un-human due to a DNA mutating disease, or from being poisoned by the venom of an unknown creature. Whatever the cause of this transformation was, they are dangerous and that is why everyone was so desperate to escape them."

"Anyway, he killed them all and by the time he was safe he knew that he wouldn't be able to use the knives ever again. He couldn't believe that he had become a killer. However, he couldn't let go of the knives. He felt he needed to keep them as a reminder of what could happen if he lost control. He died when I was six, but I will never forget him or his stories."

Alex approached us and rested his hand on And's shoulder, "No one will ever forget him, he was a great man; but right now we need rest. We have a long voyage ahead of us. We can keep watch in four hour shifts. We can all have one shift and sleep for eight hours. I want the first watch."

And and I didn't care what watch we took, so it was agreed that Alex could take the first watch. And would take the second, and I would take the last.

The second my head touched the ground I drifted off. I dreamed about what had happened recently. My arrival in Millennia is what I dreamed of the most. And, Alex, and all of their stories filled in the remaining gaps.

I knew that I was dreaming because none of it felt real; it was all familiar but none of it seemed right. The way my hair stopped reflecting the light, and the way I didn't feel the pain from my injuries were the two main reasons I knew I was sleeping.

I awoke in the middle of a nightmare. I was alone in the maze. And and Alex had left me, and I was completely lost. I ended up at the edge of a cliff, and as I peered over, my feet flew out from under me. Then, I went tumbling into darkness.

When I woke up I was sweating, and my hand was throbbing. I felt like I had just run a marathon and was in desperate need of water. My heart was racing, and I was panting so loudly that I couldn't hear myself think.

I heard a soft noise in the distance and controlled my breathing so I could hear what it was. And and Alex were both awake sitting outside the tent, and they were having a very important conversation (judging from the seriousness of their voices). I leaned closer to the entrance so I could eavesdrop on their conversation.

"This isn't good, Alex," And whispered, "We can't trust her. She is a complete stranger, and something feels strange. I feel like there's some connection between us, and I can't explain it, but it makes me want to trust her. And I shouldn't feel this way towards a stranger, so it makes me think I can't trust my instincts when I'm around her. If we can't even trust our own instincts around her, then I have no idea how we are going to survive this maze."

"Yes, we can survive," Alex argued, "We need her and she needs us. Trust your instincts, they are never wrong."

"I don't believe that," And replied, "And we will be just fine on our own. We are not very far into the maze; she will be able to make her way back to Millennia no problem. Honestly, I think that she is dead weight and we need to continue without her."

"And, do you hear what you are saying?" Alex responded, "You are saying that you want to abandon someone in the maze who is injured and knows nothing about it. Not to mention the fact that I truly do believe we need her. You're always talking about how everything happens for a reason. And I think her arrival was meant to happen. We were meant to go on this journey with her. She is going to help us in one way or another. I can feel it, and I would trust my instincts with my life."

"Fine," And spat, "but if she ends up being useless we are leaving her behind, no matter how much danger we'll be leaving her in and what our instincts are telling us to do. When it happens, and I know it will, don't say I didn't warn you."

"Deal," Alex accepted, "I know I am going to be right, and when I am; I will not waste the opportunity to say I told you so."

And playfully smacked Alex on the arm and they both started silently laughing. It made me wonder what it would be like to have a brother, but quickly fell asleep. This time I don't remember dreaming, I only remember darkness.

A sharp pain in my hand woke me up this time. And's shift was over and he was trying to wake me up so he could go to bed. The pain was so intense that I shot up and clutched my hand to make the pain go away.

"I am so sorry," And apologized, "are you alright? I will get you a new bandage to wrap your hand in." His sincere look almost made me forget about what I overheard last night…almost.

He leaned over and pulled a small cardboard box out of his bag. When he opened it, I could see that it was filled with medical supplies. He helped me up, and I stumbled out of the tent.

We didn't want to wake Alex so he took care of my hand outside. As he peeled the old bandage away from my hand I yelped in pain. He stopped and waited a minute before peeling it the rest of the way off.

My hand looked better than I had expected it to, but the skin was raw and bloody. The entire inside of the bandage had been stained red from my blood.

Blood oozed from the center of my palm, and scabs were beginning to form over the rest of my hand. The sight of it made me sick and I had to look away. And, however, didn't seem to mind.

"You don't mind blood?" I questioned.

"You are very observant," he noted before answering my question, "and no, I don't mind blood. I am hoping to become a doctor or surgeon in Millennia."

"Wow, that's really impressive," I replied.

He pulled a bottle full of clear, reflective liquid out of the box and turned it in his hands.

"This is going to sting," he warned me. I nodded and he poured a small drop into the center of my hand.

He wasn't lying. It sizzled, and my entire hand felt like it had been lit on fire. I bit my tongue to keep myself from screaming, and afterwards I tasted blood. It nearly caused me to pass out. I had seen, tasted, and lost enough blood to last me a lifetime.

I didn't realize until the pain was over that I had been gripping my forearm with my other hand. When I loosened my grip my arm was nearly purple because I had cut off the circulation, and there were small crescent-shaped cuts from where my nails had pierced through my skin.

They bled a little bit, but after all of the other injuries I had experienced it felt like nothing.

I took a few deep breaths and when I turned to look at my hand it didn't look nearly as bad. It had stopped bleeding, and most of the skin was rough instead of raw.

And gingerly bandaged it back up, and told me that it should be better within the next few days. He lightly touched my wrist and then he stealthily crawled back into the tent, and I turned to focus on the maze, but something distracted me.

My whole arm was tingling and I felt like my whole body was filled with endorphins. I couldn't help thinking about the connection And said he felt because I felt it too. It hadn't been very strong before; in fact, I wasn't even sure what I was feeling. But something clicked into place when And touched my arm. I realized it was the first time he had ever directly touched my skin without blood or anything else in the way, and it left me with a lasting impression.

When I looked down at my arm. It wasn't tingling anymore, but there was a mark forming on my wrist. Parts of my skin were darkening, and after my wrist had stopped tingling I could clearly see a double arrow ingrained in my skin.

I had no idea what it meant but I was too afraid to say anything. I had no way to know if it was good or bad. For all I knew it could be a Millennian mark of evil. I pulled the bandage on my hand up until it completely covered the mark and then I turned towards the maze in an attempt to distract myself.

All I could do was hope that the mark didn't mean

anything. I prayed it was nothing more than a side effect from the clear, reflective liquid that And had poured onto my hand. I desperately wanted to ask the brothers about it, but I decided to keep it a secret. I didn't want to take any chances.

I had been watching over the maze for less than thirty minutes when Alex appeared out of nowhere. He had been so quiet that I didn't notice him, and when he spoke I nearly tripped on my own feet.

"Sorry I startled you," he apologized, "but I wanted to talk to you."

"It-it's ok," I stammered, "So what do you want to talk about?"

"It's just...," he started, "I don't really know how to tell you this without upsetting you, but And does not want you here. He thinks that he and I should go on without you. Don't freak out, I would never leave you behind like that, but I wanted to warn you. If he is impolite and mean to you, please try not to take it personally. He is just a little...worried about traveling with a stranger, and if he doesn't get over it soon we might have to leave him behind. I know he's my brother, but I have to do what I feel is right."

"Thank you," I whispered, "I hope all of us can figure things out because if we can't trust each other we'll have no chance of surviving."

"I agree," he confirmed, "I think in the morning we should plan a strategy and try to sort through this mess."

"Sounds like a plan," I responded, "You should get some sleep; we have a long day ahead of us."

He smiled and returned to the tent. Once again I was alone. I tried not to scare myself to death, but every sound I heard or movement I saw as wind blew, and the vines on the walls moved seemed like a potential threat that was out to get me.

I would have felt much more comfortable taking the first watch when it was mainly light, but I knew that in a few hours the light would reappear and I would no longer be alone.

It was a lifetime before I saw light again. I had spent all night torturing myself by staying alert and detecting every movement and hearing any sound. The instant I saw it I darted to the tent to wake up And and Alex but paused before I walked in.

Both of them had been up more than their share last night and deserved to get some more sleep. I decided to sit at the edge and wait for them to wake up. I wrote my name over and over in the dirt as I waited.

I got the dirt out from under my nails and tried to have a thumb war with myself, but I realized after about the first five seconds that it is impossible to have a thumb war without another person. It is especially difficult when one of your hands is completely bandaged. After a while Alex emerged from the tent and sat next to me.

"We should get some breakfast," he suggested, "then we can wake up And, and set out again."

"Alright," I agreed.

We slid our packs out from the tent and sorted through them. We were looking for something to eat, and luckily it wasn't hard to find. We each had some trail mix and a glass of water for breakfast.

When we were finished, I was still hungry, and I was certain that Alex felt the same way. However, we were going to have to get used to this kind of hunger because we had only packed a week or so worth of food.

I leaned onto my elbow and cringed when I heard my back crack. It had never been that loud before. When I stood and stretched out my arms, my knees and elbows cracked, too.

I slid the blanket across the rope, but the light didn't even make And roll in the other direction. He just stayed where he was, as unmoving as a corpse.

"He's the hardest person in the world to wake up," Alex stated. He shook And back and forth for nearly a minute before And shot up with his hand glued to the knife at his waist.

"You scared the life out of me," he complained.

"It's not my fault that you sleep like the dead," Alex stated.

"Ugh," And groaned and rolled over onto his stomach.

"You need to get up," Alex joked, "if you don't, we might just leave you behind to get eaten." Alex and I laughed until we were crying, and when we finally stopped And got to his feet and rubbed his eyes.

"Time to pack up camp," And sighed and began untying the ropes from the vines. Alex and I slid the blankets off the rope and sloppily folded them before storing them in our backpacks.

When And finally untied the knots in the rope he

wound it around his hand and shoved it into the front pocket of his backpack. Alex and I held up the edges of the blanket that had been on the ground and And smacked it with the back of his hand until it was nearly dirt-free.

We folded it and stored it with the rest of our supplies. The whole process took fifteen or twenty minutes, but I had a feeling that we were going to get much faster at it if we were moving camp every day.

"Well, it's time to start moving," And huffed. We walked out from our little isolated section of the maze, and soon we were back into the main part of the maze. Four tunnels stared at us, two were directly in front of us and there was one on either side of us.

Without any hesitation And walked towards the one in front of us. It was slightly to the left. Alex and I followed but we were more hesitant.

It was odd how And seemed to know exactly where he was going because all of the maze maps had been destroyed years ago. The brief pause left about twenty feet between where And was and where Alex and I were.

"How is he so certain about where he's going?" I asked Alex.

"Either he's a genius, who knows everything, or he's following the same turns he and Kate took. My guess is the second one. I also think that the real reason he came with us was because he still wants to find her. Kind of like how we want to find our sisters."

"Oh," I replied in surprise.

"Yeah," he said, "That's part of the reason why I said we might eventually have to leave him behind. I can't trust him, even if he is my own brother, because he has this weird thing against you for no reason. You two have not even had a conversation when I wasn't around, so I know that you didn't do anything to him. I also feel like he has a different goal than us, and he might jeopardize our success for his own. It's all just very confusing."

"Yeah," I agreed.

We had to jog to catch up with And before the next turn. This time we turned right, and again there was no hesitation as And chose what way to turn. Alex and I fell behind again, and this repeated several times but each time we turned a new direction.

I began to wonder if he had memorized all these turns or if he was guessing. The less hesitation he had, the more mine grew. I was skeptical because he wasn't here for the same reason as Alex and me. What if he was leading us into a death trap?

If he was taking us the way he had gone with Kate it meant we were most likely heading in the direction of danger. I was just about to ask Alex what his opinion was when we all stopped. In front of us was an enormous gate.

It was taller than the maze walls themselves, and it was a rusted, gold color. The bars along the top formed a pair of wings, and the rest of it was a maze of bars going in every direction. We couldn't climb over it because the top was lined with sharp spikes. We were going to have to climb under it.

"How the heck are we going to pass this thing?" Alex wondered aloud.

"We have to dig under it," I explained.

"Do you know how long that will take us?" Alex complained.

"It's the only way," And stated, "last night I looked around a little while I was on watch, and all of the other paths are dead ends. This is our only option."

"Oh," Alex muttered, "but it is still going to take forever."

"Not if we work together," I reminded him, "Teamwork can make or break anything."

"I guess we are about to find out," Alex agreed, "where do we start?"

"The far side," I suggested, it's the least expected spot for someone to break through. That means the ground shouldn't be as difficult to break there."

"Let's get started," Alex smirked at And as if to say 'I told you so.' And rolled his eyes in response. I knew that their conversation from last night was more than a logical debate, it was a competition.

We all crouched down at the far corner, and our hands began to sift through the dirt on the surface and brush it away. After we had dug five or six centimeters the dirt started to become thicker and it stuck to our hands like sap in the spring.

Within minutes we were all dirty and sticky. Dirt covered my face. Every time I brushed my hair away from my face, or wiped sweat from my forehead it would get worse.

We were going to need a new plan. The dirt and mud were too dense to dig through; not to mention the gate continued into the ground, and made it nearly impossible to get past it from underneath. We checked all along the bottom of the fence to make sure there weren't any openings we had missed. We didn't get lucky.

Alex and And sat leaning against the gate while I paced back and forth in front of them. I felt like a teacher getting ready to punish two naughty children. I couldn't help it though, I needed to concentrate. Even more importantly I had to find a way past this obstacle, so I could prove to And that they needed me here just as much as they needed each other, or possibly more.

"Will you stop that," And criticized, "I can't think while you are doing that, it is so distracting." I couldn't tell if he was angry at me or the fact that he couldn't figure out the puzzle.

"Whatever," I spat, and I rolled my eyes at him. Then I went and sat on the other side of Alex.

"So we can't go over it, and we can't go under it," And thought aloud, "what other options does that leave us with?"

"What about through or around?" I spoke too soon, and I wished I could take back what I had said. Stupid comments were not going to earn me any respect from And, and they were certainly not going to prove that I was needed. I wanted to slap myself for being such an idiot.

"That is one of the stupidest ideas I have ever heard. Oh, and trust me, I have heard a lot of them in my lifetime;" And critiqued, "but, yours might just be insane and illogical enough to work. The fence is solid and doesn't have a latch anywhere, so I don't know how we could possibly get through it. But we might be able to go around it. No matter what happens, we have to remember that every obstacle in this maze has one solution, and it is not going to be as obvious as we would like it to be sometimes." I wasn't sure if that was meant to be a compliment or an insult, but it seemed like he was making an effort.

"Okay," I beamed, "Let's get through this gate before it gets dark again. Then we will have plenty of time to set up camp and rest."

"Sounds good to me," Alex chimed in, "Where should we start?"

"We should try to loosen the strength in the walls. We can do this by throwing our weight against it. Then we can push away the parts that break off and climb through an opening to the other side. Finally, we can cover it up so that it will be hidden, and we will be able to use it again if we need to." And and Alex both nodded in agreement with the plan.

We got into a line in front of the wall and charged toward it. We hit the hard surface with the side of our shoulders. The second I connected I stumbled backwards, and fell onto my knees.

My shoulder ached, and I watched as a purple and blue bruise spread over the surface. I watched Alex take his first hit, and he stumbled backwards but didn't fall.

When And hit it he only shook, and his feet stayed firmly planted on the ground the whole time. I glanced at their shoulders to see if they were as injured as mine, but only a small section - smaller than the size of my fingertips - was bruised.

We all stumbled back to the fence and slumped

against it in defeat. I had been wrong, again. My luck was running out, and it was taking my confidence with it.

"I guess we are going to have to get through it, even though I have no idea how that's at all possible," And spoke up, "But we still have to try because if we can't get past this we'll have to backtrack, and then we'll end up wasting valuable time. I think we should all search the gate for anything that could be a latch or lever to open it. My guess is that it will be hidden in the mess of bars, or it might be at the top. The only thing we can be certain of is if there is a latch or lever it will be harder to find than a needle in a haystack."

"Let's begin," I said in serious voice.

We stood side-by-side along the fence, and searched for any hidden thing that could open it. I scanned the top, Alex searched through the bars, and And crouched on the ground looking for something at the bottom. I stepped back so I could get a better view of the top. That's when I noticed it. The bars in the middle weren't placed randomly. They were a puzzle.

"And, Alex!" I screamed in delight, "I think I figured it out! The bars are like a puzzle. We have to move them around to make a certain pattern, and then the gate will open. Or maybe there will be an opening for us to fit through."

"You are a genius!" Alex smiled, "I never would have thought of that."

"Neither would I," And grumbled, "Congratulations, I think you have solved the first roadblock." Looking at his jealous face made me feel like I was on cloud nine. Maybe I was meant to be here. I felt like I could finally stop doubting myself.

"Thanks," I beamed. Although it wasn't much of a compliment it was an improvement, and I finally felt like he was beginning to accept me.

"Let's start!" Alex cheered. He was always the most enthusiastic out of us all.

"Hold your horses." I knew that And was holding back. He didn't usually have much patience when he thought someone was being careless. "We need to make a plan first, because if we just start randomly moving things, it's going to become more tangled than it was to start with."

"K, ok..," Alex sighed. I could tell that he was sick of planning, and this was not the adventure he was hoping for.

I spoke up and said, "We should move them all in one direction: all to the right, the left, up, down, or like away from the middle."

"We should move them all down, leaving an opening at the top because that is what will be least expected for us to do. We will have to find a way to reach the opening then, but it isn't impossible, and I think we can figure it out," And suggested.

"Okay," I agreed, "Let's start."

As it turned out I was right. The bars slid in the direction that we pushed them. The first few were hard to push because they had been nearly rusted in place, but eventually they loosened and were fairly easy to move.

We had to push our entire weight against them, and even then some of them didn't budge. We followed our plan and pulled them all towards the bottom, but that didn't last for long.

Some of the bars moved back and forth, some moved at an angle, and some moved up and down. However, they all only moved in one direction, so it was impossible to pull them all towards the bottom. We needed a new "attack plan."

"Maybe they all spread away from the middle," And stated, "that would make sense."

"Yeah," I responded, "but it makes too much sense, and I don't think that the designers would do something that was so obvious."

"True," Alex commented, "It needs to be something unique; something people would not think of."

"What if it makes a pattern?" I guessed, "Is there anything unique about Millennia's history which could be displayed as like a pattern or picture?"

"A torch," And and Alex answered at the same time.

"That makes sense," I agreed, "hopefully plan number four will be lucky." And and Alex gave a small nod in my direction, and we immediately started to work.

We slid the bars back and forth trying to create the general shape of a torch, but every time it looked more like an ice cream cone than a torch.

We took turns standing back and watching the process, telling who to move what bar where. This system sped up the process, and every time we switched people it looked more and more like a torch.

Right as And and Alex were switching positions I realized there was a bar that had not been moved yet. It was directly above my head, and when I reached my hand up, my fingertips barely brushed the surface.

I stood on the tip of my toes and stretched towards the bar. I wrapped my hand around it, and it felt different from the rest of the bars.

I ran my hand along it slowly, that way I wouldn't miss anything different about it. When my hand had nearly reached the end it bumped into something sharp. I yelped in pain. And and Alex rushed over.

"What happened?" they asked.

I pointed to the bar above me and said, "There's something sharp at the end of that bar and it stabbed my hand." I turned my hand over to show them the cut.

"It's a very minor cut; I am sure it will heal within the next few hours, and the pain will go away any minute," And assured me, "What I am worried about is what is on the back of that bar."

"There's only one way find out," Alex interjected.

"Yes," And began, "Alex, I will lift you up so you can see what it is." Alex nodded and climbed onto And's back. When And stood Alex was at the perfect height to see behind the bar.

"Oh, my gosh!" Alex exclaimed. His voice reminded me of an overly dramatic teenage girl getting a brand new car for her birthday.

"What!" And and I cried.

Alex turned around grinning and said, "The thing that poked you is a lever, and I am guessing that when I pull it, this gate will open." We all shrieked with pleasure, and I felt pride in being the one who had noticed the bar didn't move. I was also the one to question the fact that it was slightly thicker than the rest.

"Well, you should feel lucky for finding something useful. If you hadn't, I totally would have called you out on how girly you just sounded," And teased. Alex blushed, and all I could think to do was turn away from the situation.

Alex thrust down on the lever, but nothing happened. We all stood there waiting. I was just about to ask Alex if he had pulled down hard enough when there was a long, sharp creak.

The gate didn't swing open as we had all anticipated; instead all the bars began to move a million miles an hour in every direction.

Just watching the speed in which they moved made me dizzy, and I had to turn around. When the sound of metal sliding back and forth finally stopped I turned back towards the gate.

The opening in the gate was the shape of the number one. We had just passed the first roadblock, and who knows how many more we would encounter. At least next time we would know what to expect.

CHAPTER IV
ALEX

We staggered toward the gate. It was glowing so brightly that you could feel the blazing heat from miles away. The smoke and ash surrounding it was infinite, and the air tasted like burnt popcorn. The opening was shaped like the number one, and it was so narrow that I had to suck in my stomach to pass through.

When I was almost through the side of my hand grazed the burning metal bars, and I bit my tongue to avoid hollering in pain. Erin had no problem fitting through the opening, and she did it in a matter of seconds.

And, on the other hand, had more trouble because he couldn't fit through without touching the bars. Erin and I had to pull him through, and afterwards he crumpled to the ground. His skin was raw and covered in burns. The smoke had become so dense that we couldn't walk. Instead we had to crawl.

And was weak, and Erin and I had to lay him across our backs. When we reached the end of the smoke Erin and I immediately began tending And's wounds.

At this point he was unconscious. His clothes were torn and burned, and his skin was stained with blood and peeling. Erin and I had never had to care for a burn this serious, so we just poured water along his skin and hoped for the best.

"Do you think that he is going to be okay?" I looked to Erin for reassurance.

"I don't know," she admitted, "I've never seen a burn that was this serious, and we don't have proper medical supplies. He'll probably live, but in what condition I'm not sure."

I nodded and asked, "How did you know that that bar would open the gate?"

"I didn't," she confessed, "We just hadn't moved it before, and it was thicker than the rest, so I decided to give it a shot because it wasn't like we had anything to lose."

"Are you nervous about the next roadblock yet?" I knew that I was asking a lot of questions, but I think that getting opinions from other people is comforting.

"Somewhat," she contemplated what to say next, "We passed this one, so I feel confident; but the next one could be way harder. And if they keep getting more challenging, then I'm not sure if we're going to make it..," she trailed off.

I turned up the corner of my mouth as if I was telling her I felt the same, and afterwards we did nothing but sit and wait. We waited for And to wake up, for the smoke to reach us, and for a miracle to happen that would let us know everything was going to be okay.

I imagined what things would be like if I hadn't gone with Erin into the maze. Would I be taking a walk with And? Would I be wondering what was going to happen tomorrow? Would I be waiting for something to magically change my life?

Although Erin's arrival had led to danger and pain, I knew that it was better than my life was before. She had changed everything, and given me such a different view of the world.

My parents had talked again. It felt like I finally had a family again, and I wasn't waiting anymore. I used to think that if I waited long enough something would happen, and it would change the way things were. I was taking everything one day at a time and never enjoying myself.

I realized that since Ria had left, I had been just letting my life waste away. I never took charge of anything, and I didn't want to. I had shut people out because I thought things would be easier that way. In reality, those things did nothing but make my life lonely and miserable. I decided from then on, I was going to stop waiting and start living.

I started shaking And. He needed to wake up so we could continue. I saw Erin open her mouth to protest, but at the last minute she stopped herself. It was as if she read my mind, and realized that we had to find a way to wake up And so we could continue.

"Ugh…" And groaned.

"Come on, And, you need to get up now," I insisted, "If you don't Erin and I might just go on without you."

"You wouldn't," he opened his eyes, and challenged me.

"Watch me," I got up and began walking further down the tunnel, Erin was right behind me.

"OKAY!" And called, "I get it. I am getting up, please just wait a minute. I need to catch up with you." I paused and turned around wondering if he was lying or not.

Sure enough, he was up and hobbling in our direction. He had his hands on his stomach to cover a long, thick gash. Blood was caking his hands and stomach. When he reached Erin and me he crumpled to the ground again.

We tied a shirt around his stomach to stop the blood from flowing from the gash, and he stood between Erin and me. He used our shoulders to support himself. When we came to the next "intersection" And murmured, "Go right."

We did as he said, and then we walked in that direction until we nearly collapsed from exhaustion. We had reached a broken, old, crumbling bridge. All of the boards on the bottom were either cracked or missing, and the ropes holding everything together looked frail and tattered.

The distance beneath the bridge went on forever, and all you could see was darkness. After the first bridge there was an outline of a second bridge, but it was too far away for me to determine the condition of it.

I told Erin and And to stay a few feet away from the bridge, meanwhile I planned to examine its stability. When I approached it, it looked like it was going to crumple at any second. The bridges had to be the second roadblock, but they were very different from the first. This obstacle was dangerous, and if you failed you died. There was no such thing as second chances.

When I went back to tell Erin and And about the bridges they were both asleep. Erin's head was on And's chest, and she held a cloth in her hand. She had probably been about to clean the blood off of him when she fell asleep. I assumed this meant I was taking the first watch. I didn't mind because I wasn't as tired as they were, and it gave me time to think about the bridges.

We didn't have anything we could use to make them safe, and they would most likely only hold one person at a time. We were going to have to trust them to hold us, and hope for the best.

Just before sleep took control of my body I shook Erin awake so she could take the second watch. I would have made And do it, but for the past few hours she had been murmuring in her sleep.

I assumed that she was having a nightmare and thought that taking watch would be a good way for her to clear her head. When she woke up she gave me a grateful smile. She started to say something, but my brain shut down and I was knocked out into a deep sleep.

At first my dreams seemed pleasant, but they all eventually turned into nightmares. I was walking across the bridge, and behind me I heard a faint, desperate scream. I hadn't realized that the board below me was breaking.

I turned and saw Erin's worried eyes, and that's the last thing I saw before plunging into darkness. My sides were bloody from the boards ripping through my flesh.

Below me there was no sign of a bottom to the cliff. At last I woke with And and Erin hovering over me.

And had a worried face that mixed with a sense of relief when my eyes fluttered open. As usual, Erin's face was a white wall. My arm had been covered by a wet cloth and my fingernails were stained with blood. When I peeled away the cloth there was a shallow cut running from my elbow to my wrist.

All of the blood had been cleaned from And, and there was a clean bandage wrapped around his torso. There were only a few major cuts on the rest of his body, and lots of small scrapes covering his skin. He was more scabs and cuts then he was human flesh.

"What happened?" Erin choked.

"What do you mean?" I questioned.

"You-you were screaming for help, and you clawed through your skin," she shuddered.

"Oh," I glanced back down at my arm and saw four straight lines, and then I looked at my fingernails. Dried blood and pieces of dead skin were stuck to and under them.

This time it was And who spoke, "Alex," he said softly, "What happened? Why did you do this to yourself?"

"I don't know," I admitted, "I was having a nightmare, and I must have been gripping my arm so hard that I tore skin..," I trailed off. And looked even more worried than before.

"What happened in the dream?" he hesitated.

"I was walking across the bridge," I began, "and then the board below me broke. When I fell it slashed at my skin, and it broke through the surface. I was looking down, but I could not see the bottom of the cliff. I-I thought I was going to die. Then I woke up with a bloody arm, and it felt like someone had knocked the wind out of me." I shut my eyes and buried my face in my hands.

"It's all good," And's soothing voice reminded me of when I was a little boy. Whenever I was hurt or had a bad dream he would always tell me how everything was going to be okay. He promised he would never let anything happen to me.

"Yeah," Erin piped up, "And said the cut was shallow; it will probably go away within a day or so." Her smile was warm and inviting, but at the same time it was forced and emotionless.

I tried to read her real expression, but as always there was no hint of emotion. I returned her smile and gazed at the bridge. I wondered what it would be like if I could tell what she was thinking, but her mind was a puzzle that had no solution. I began to think of other things, but thoughts of Erin lingered in my mind.

And turned to see where I was looking and divulged, "I wish there was another way to go, but while I was on watch I searched. Everything else is a dead end."

"It's okay, it was just a dream. I know it wasn't real," I lied. The dream seemed more real than ever, I was afraid it was a vision of the future. And gave me a sympathetic look before turning to face Erin. He knew I was lying.

"I guess that it's time for us to come up with a plan," I was trying to be positive, but my voice shook with fear.

And immediately began to rattle off his plan, "First things first. I can see four different bridges, and there are platforms separating them from one another. Obviously the first bridge is broken, but we have no idea how the rest of them are going to challenge us.

I suggest that we go one at a time across the broken bridge. We will have a rope tied to the ankle that is being held by someone else. This way, if we fall we won't die. The rope will be there to catch us.

We have two ropes. This means that the first two people will go using separate ropes. Then, the last person can use one of the ropes someone else used. When we are all at the platform we can see what the next bridge is. From there, we can modify the plan or make a new one."

No one objected, and we decided Erin would go first. This was because she was lightest. Therefore, she would break the least amount of boards. I would go next, and And would go last. For the first time ever I thought I could sense how Erin was feeling.

She looked nervous. She was playing with her hair, and twisting it around her finger. When she took her first step onto the bridge we were all holding our breath.

When the board held I felt my pulse slow. This still didn't stop my heart from pounding in my head. When she reached the platform not a single board had broken.

She took a bow and turned to sit on the platform. She had made it across easily and quickly. I guess I wasn't getting any better at reading her emotions. I took my first step onto the bridge, and it let out a long, distressed creak. I froze. Mentally I was preparing myself for the long fall ahead of me, but it never came.

I took another step, and the bridge began to sway. I stumbled for a few feet before I grabbed onto a piece of rope. At one point it was meant to be a railing, but now it was frail and only partially attached to the bridge. Dust covered my hands, and the boards screamed with every movement I made.

My hands were sticky from sweat. My lungs were gasping for air. I shuffled from board to board without looking up. I was afraid I would fall if I took my eyes off of my feet. I needed to go one step at a time. If I tried to think ahead I would falter.

I was fairly certain I looked like a fish in a parking lot, clumsy and out of place. I envied Erin for being so graceful. She made it look as easy as breathing. She had done it a million times, and her mind didn't even need to think about it anymore.

When I reached the edge of the bridge I leaped onto the platform. I couldn't believe I was still alive. None of the boards had broken either. Their bark was much worse than their bite.

They were a lot stronger than we thought they were. However, their strength was about to be put to the test. And was like a rock. He was strong and stable, one shell full of pure muscle. This also caused him to be much heavier than he looked. Hopefully his speed would make up for it.

He took his first step, and the board squealed in pain. On his second step he wasn't as lucky. The board held for a few seconds, but then it snapped in half. And caught the next board, and he tried to pull himself up. His muscles were showing through his shirt, but his hands slipped at the last second.

I stood frozen in horror as And plunged into the darkness. I heard his scream explode like fireworks. It was desperate and helpless. I braced myself to catch him.

The rope finally came to an end. It stretched so far I worried it would snap in half. My feet flew out from under me. My rear end smashed into the platform, and I let out a deep groan. The impact almost caused me to drop the rope.

I felt a pair of hands on my shoulder, and I turned around to see Erin pulling me off the ground. I leaned back and pulled my knees to my chest. I carefully leaned forward and got to my feet. Erin kept her hands on my shoulders, and she slowly dragged me towards the middle of the platform.

My ears were ringing and my vision was spinning. My fingers were turning white, but I didn't dare loosen my grip. Erin called something out, but the words were lost in the air. Soon after, she pushed me onto the ground and sat behind me. I fell onto my stomach, but I was too distracted to feel any pain.

She wrapped her arms around me to keep me steady. I turned my head to ask her what she was doing, but my question was answered without her help. The rope started swaying and shaking in my hands. She had been calling to And, and he was starting to climb up.

I leaned up onto my elbows to make myself more stable. I focused on my breathing. This helped me forget about the rope. It was constantly becoming harder and harder to hold onto. Every time And advanced, the rope was pulled further out of my hands. What I still held onto became heavier, and my struggling grew.

I didn't realize And had made it to the platform until I felt Erin's hands lift. I opened my eyes. They hurt because I had been squeezing them shut for such a long time. The air I had kept trapped in my lungs for so long was finally released. The muscles in my chest and face finally started to relax.

My vision was blurred, and it felt like everything around me was moving. Slowly my eyes adjusted, and my vision began to sharpen. Soon I could see everything clearly. Erin and And's faces were bright red. They were breathing hard, and all I could hear was the sound of them panting.

My fingers finally spread apart, and the rope slid out between them. I stretched out my arms and my elbows made a loud cracking noise. The blood was finally coming back to my fingertips, and they were returning to their normal color.

My palms were rope-burned, but it wasn't an extensive injury. The worst it could do was make my hands sore. Even then, it would only last for the next few days. And had a few shallow cuts running along the side of his arms and legs, but those were his only visible injuries. He had been scared mentally more so than physically.

I can safely say this event frightened us all. At least we were fortunate enough to have avoided any severe physical damage. We were still recovering from previous injuries as well as those from the last obstacle.

At first I thought we had passed the second roadblock, but then I remembered. We still had three more bridges to cross. I turned towards the next section. I felt like I had just been hit in the face with a sack of flour.

The second bridge looked safer than the first one at first, but stability was not what I was worried about this time. There was a complicated pattern covering the floor. It was made up of spikes, daggers, and swords.

Some routes looked easier than others, but none of those could be taken. They all had steps that were slightly higher than the rest. Those steps triggered a blade. The blade would cut through a rope; if that happened you were in for a surprise.

A variety of weapons would fall from the ceiling. They would swing back and forth in an attempt to decapitate you. If that didn't happen, a spear would pierce your skull. No matter what happened, your odds of living would go right out the window. Higher ground needed to be avoided.

I looked to Erin and And. I longed to see a flame of hope or desire in their eyes, but both of them were busy staring at the bridge. And's mouth was hanging wide open, and Erin's head was tilted to the side. The only fire left in me flickered until fear blew it out.

There was no turning back now. No matter how intimidated I was, the road turning back was damaged. The only option left was forward. All we needed was sixty seconds. Sixty seconds of bravery. If we could find it, we would live to see another day.

Strategies were not discussed. Plans were not even

thought about. Everything was random. All we could do now was be brave and hope for the best. Adrenaline was pumping through my body. I was ready. I was going to be courageous.

I only took a few moments to plan my route before I set off. My mind wasn't controlling my body. I didn't need to think about what to do, I knew. The path I chose was mainly straight, but I would have to take a few small detours to avoid higher areas.

The spacing between the weapons was narrow. I had to walk on my toes to avoid stepping on them. My calves burned, and my face was covered in a mask of sweat. I started to panic, this lead me to make a crucial mistake.

I rubbed my eyes, which caused me to step on a small dagger. Over an inch of the cold metal sunk into my heel. I wailed in pain, but it wasn't loud enough to be heard. I pulled my knee up, but the dagger was stuck. It was glued to my foot.

When Erin and And realized what was happening they raced toward me. Their eyes were like magnets, and they were attracted to me. They paid no attention to where they were stepping, and they hadn't noticed some of the ground being higher. They didn't even look down for a split second.

And's face was sheer panic and determination. It was like he was trying to save his own life. Erin's eyes were wide. She was watching all around her. She knew exactly where she was stepping and where she wanted to be. I swear she never blinked.

What happened didn't seem like a very big deal to

me. I wondered if I was missing something. Maybe something bad had happened on the platform and they needed to get away. This sounded like the most logical explanation to me.

I suddenly became even more desperate to free myself. I pulled my foot up with all of my strength, but no amount of force was stronger than the grip of the dagger. I felt like I was trying to cut through a steel cable with a plastic spoon.

As they neared the higher ground I called out a warning to them. The only problem was, no sound came out from my mouth. As a result swords dropped from the ceiling, and long blades began to swing back and forth. It was a combination of both terrible things I had foreseen.

Call me a pessimist, but I was expecting the worst. I was waiting for something bad to happen. I was shocked when it never came. The way they weaved through the path and dodged the obstacles was nothing more than a game of hopscotch.

They reached me in a matter of seconds. Erin stumbled towards the end, so she was slightly behind And. He tried to lift me off of the dagger, but the glue held strong. I was nervous but at the same time I felt less embarrassed. I thought I couldn't free myself because I was too weak, but if And couldn't help no one could.

He slipped his knife into his hand with one swift motion. Then he began trying to cut the dagger away from the bridge. Erin had finally reached us, and she immediately began to help. She slowly maneuvered around me and began cutting away at the dagger from the other side.

A soft rubbery material was what held the dagger to the bridge. And and Erin separated the dagger from the bridge in a matter of minutes. The second they had finished, everything in the room started to spin. Black dots formed in the corner of my eyes, and they slowly started to grow.

And slung me across his shoulder and started racing across the rest of the bridge. He was like a fireman saving a small child from a burning building. My eyes were losing in the battle they fought against the blackness. The last thing I saw was a long, silver blade. It was slicing through the air. The target it was aiming for was Erin's face.

I was completely unaware of what was happening when we reached the next platform. My mind was completely numb and it didn't want to think. The only thing I felt was a frigid metal surface beneath me. I leaned my face against it, and closed my eyes. When I opened them the dots in my vision were absent, and only returned momentarily when I blinked.

I was torn between sitting up and staying where I was. As much as I knew I couldn't, I wanted to lay there forever. The cool surface felt good, like I had just flipped my pillow over in the middle of the night. My eyes were heavy, and I didn't have the strength to keep them open anymore.

I was just about to let my eyelids slip shut when I remembered. The blade was headed straight for Erin's face. It was just about to hit her between the eyes when my vision went black. My eyelids snapped back open. I shot up, and I immediately felt dizzy.

I felt a hand on my back. It felt strong and stable, so I was certain it was And. I turned around to ask him what happened to Erin, but I had been wrong. Erin was the one who kept me upright. Something about her looked different, but I wasn't sure what it was.

Finally it hit me. Her hair was much shorter. Now it ended in the middle of her neck, and it was cleanly cut. The blade must have sliced through it while she was running. If she had been a second later she would be dead.

"I'm totally loving the new hairstyle," I teased her.

"Oh shut up," she laughed. She smiled and smacked me playfully on the arm. "I'm just happy that my head isn't lying in the middle of that bridge right now. It was almost sliced clean off by one of those blades."

"Would that have really been a bad thing?" And joked.

"Uh yes, I can't even imagine how much of a pain cleaning that up would be..," Erin looked at And with dagger eyes, "I think we should start thinking about getting past the next bridge. Being on this platform is starting to really creep me out, and I'm not really in the mood for talking about how much you would enjoy my death."

After that And lifted Erin up. His hands held onto her waist, and he tilted her forward. She was dangling over the platform, and he pretended to drop her over the edge. Erin screamed at the top of her lungs, and And let his hands slip until he was holding her by the ankles.

"It's not that I'm not enjoying this," I taunted, "but I'm afraid her screaming is going burst my eardrums." And set Erin down, and she stuck her tongue out at him while making a sour face.

"Now that you know what I'm capable of doing, I suggest you don't give me a reason to hang you over the platform again. Who knows, next time you might end up slipping out of my hands..," And grinned and winked.

Erin rolled her eyes in response and the corners of her mouth were slightly tilted upward. I never would have noticed it if I hadn't been standing in the exact place I was.

"Moving on," she began, "How the heck are we going to cross this bridge, because I for one am not very coordinated on, you know, ice..,"

I looked at the bridge, and for the first time I realized that it was a long sheet of ice. It was perfectly smooth. The top layer wasn't quite solid, but it wasn't liquid either. At least now I knew why the platform was so cold.

"There's no need to worry, sweetie," And claimed, "I am the master of being coordinated on ice."

"Um, And, there's no ice in Millennia. So I do not really see how you could be master of that..," I reminded him.

"It's not my fault that there isn't," And stated, "Regardless, if there was ice in Millennia, I would totally be a master when it came to getting across it."

"Sure..," I replied. And scolded me as if he was telling me to shut up.

"Well, I guess we're going to find out," Erin interjected.

"Yes, we will," And said confidently.

He stalked over towards the ice and started walking

across the bridge. His hands were shaking, but the way he moved his arms made it nearly impossible to notice. After he had walked a few yards he turned around.

"Told you so," he smirked, "I am already a fourth of the way across, and I haven't slipped once." His voice cracked at first, but then it was smooth as silk.

"You still have seventy-five percent of the way left to go," Erin pointed out. She raised her eyebrows and shrugged her shoulders. I think she was trying to hide how impressed she was. I for one was amazed at And's balance and coordination on the ice.

Erin stood up and started walking towards the bridge. When she reached it she paused and tapped the surface with her foot before stepping onto it. She took her time as she shuffled along the ice towards And. Her feet didn't dare lift from the ground.

The amount of time it took for me to reach them felt like an eternity. The next few moments, however, did not pass as slowly. Soon after I reached them we heard a sound. It sounded like glass shattering.

I turned around, and the front of the bridge was cracking. It looked like a newly woven spider web, and if I wasn't in danger I would have thought it was beautiful. My eyes wanted to watch the cracks expand, but my brain forced me to look away.

Erin and And had already started running. I knew there was no chance of me being able to catch up to them. The pain in my foot was manageable, but I was still walking with a limp. I would be lucky if I made it to the last platform in time.

I half limped and half ran. I'm sure I looked ridiculous, but doing something embarrassing was not what I was afraid of. The floor below me was shaking, and as it increased I knew my time was running out.

When I looked up to see if Erin and And had made it to safety yet, I saw And crawling on his hands and knees. He must have fallen somewhere along the way. He was a confused dog that had no way of keeping its balance.

He nearly shoved Erin onto the platform, and then he turned around and started running towards me. He used the edge of the platform to push himself up. It looked like he was just starting a race in a track meet.

Erin didn't seem very happy about being shoved onto the platform. She stood for a second with her mouth wide open. Then she slid her feet across the edge of the platform (to get the melted ice off of the bottom of her shoes) and started chasing after And.

And reached me in record time, and Erin was on his heels. And picked me up, and Erin helped him carry me to the platform. We were going much faster than I was before. Speed was of the essence, and I was grateful for the improvement.

I glanced down to see how much the ice had cracked, and my stomach dropped. The front part of the bridge was no longer there, and more and more was rapidly disappearing. Our margin of error was slowly fading. And and Erin seemed to notice, too. They quickened their pace.

We were only a few yards away, and the ice was right on our heels. And reached the platform. Erin was just about to step onto it when the ice below her feet broke. She instinctively released me and tried to get ahold of the edge.

And sat me on the ground, and he turned his attention to Erin. She was holding onto the platform with one hand, and her fingers were slipping. And wrapped his hand around her wrist right as her last finger slipped. I didn't want to watch. My eyes missed him catching her, and I thought she had died.

When I looked back, And was lying on his stomach. His arm was outstretched over the side of the platform. I let out the air that I had been holding prisoner in my lungs. Time had stopped, but now the clock was ticking again. I looked forward, and waited for And to pull Erin up from the side of the platform.

I stretched my feet out in front of me, and I realized my foot had been bandaged. I must have fallen asleep while my vision was black. I had almost certainly overlooked the bandages when I woke up. I had been so fascinated with Erin's newly shortened hair, and it was like I was wearing blinders.

I felt stupid. Something as simple as a person's hair kept me from noticing my foot had been bandaged. I had never seen a girl with short hair before, but it shouldn't have been such a shock. In Millennia girls kept their hair so long it brushed their hips when they walked, but many of them would wind it into intricate buns to keep it out of their faces.

And still hadn't pulled Erin up. I knew something was wrong. A shiver went up my spine. I slid next him and glanced down at the scene below. Again, I was afraid Erin had died. Luckily I was wrong again. When I looked down all I saw was blackness, and Erin.

And must have not been strong enough to pull her up (I'm guessing it had something to do with him lying on his stomach). Erin was slowly moving her hands up his arms. I wasn't sure why that would be so hard, but then I realized she couldn't get past his elbow. Whenever she reached it, she ended up slipping back down. At the last minute she would catch his fingertips and have to restart.

I lowered myself onto my stomach like And had done. I stretched my arm towards Erin. She was holding onto And's hand like it was her own life, and it was. She shook as she released one of her hands and grabbed onto mine.

And was now able to move onto his knees, and I did the same. Erin's hands were finally at the same height as the platform. And grabbed onto her wrists with both of his hands and I let go of her. He slowly stood up, and pulled her onto the platform.

Her face was red from exhaustion, and she was shaking. And put his arm around her and whispered something into her ear. I couldn't tell what he said, but I assumed that it was one of his snide but witty comments because she smiled and rolled her eyes.

She leaned back until her back was flat against the platform. She stayed there for a few seconds before she got to her feet. And helped her walk to the middle of the platform. She was still shaking from fear, and we all sat in dead silence while our brains processed what had happened.

"Thank you," Erin croaked, "I wouldn't be alive if it wasn't for you."

She smiled, but this time was different from all the others. Her smile was usually cold and forced, but this one was full of warmth. It made my soul smile, and I wanted to hold onto it forever.

"No problem," And replied, "I know you would have done the same thing if it had happened to Alex or me.

"I am actually the one that should be thanking you two," I reminded them, "If it was not for me, you would not have almost died. And if it was not for you two, I would be dead. So, uh thanks," I smiled.

"Like And said," Erin replied, "it's no problem, I'm sure you would have done the same thing if it had been one of us out there. By the way, how is your foot feeling? We gave you some painkillers and bandaged it, but I don't know how much it really helped."

"It's actually a lot better, thank you for asking," I answered.

"Anytime," Erin noted, "It doesn't look like the maze is meant to cause permanent damage. Even though you lost a lot of blood and passed out for a while, your foot healed way faster than normal. Also, when And got burned, it left him looking sunburned. And there was no further damage. The only permanent damage it can cause is death."

"That actually makes sense," And agreed, "At least now we know we won't ever be seriously hurt, but like you said, the maze is meant to kill. We still need to use extreme caution, and there are no excuses not to. Now, do you have an idea that will get us across the last bridge? One that won't, well, burn us to death..," he trailed off.

"WOW!" Erin exaggerated, "And doesn't have an idea? I didn't think that was possible."

I was absolutely positive; this final stretch was going to be the longest and hardest one. The bridge was solid black because it was covered in ashes. Rings of fire lined the middle and edges of the bridge, and fire would shoot up out of the floor at random places and times.

It appeared to be impossible to cross without being scorched. And shuddered every time he looked at it, and I knew that he hadn't forgotten about what happened at the gate.

The burn marks had mostly vanished. The only remains of them were his sunburned- looking skin. He also had two long, faded, white scars. They ran from his knees down to a few inches above his ankles. They were a quarter of an inch thick, and the ends were forked.

Erin put her arm around And, and gave him a thoughtful look then whispered, "Everything is going to be alright." He responded by smiling and brushing his lips across the top of her head. The gesture was small, but it spoke for itself.

All of our eyes were glued to the fire. It was as beautiful as fireworks, and as terrible as murder. I focused. I wanted to find some sort of pattern. Thus far I had been the most useless, and I needed to start pulling my own weight.

After a few moments Erin let her arm drop. And pulled his knees towards himself, and wrapped his arms around them to keep his balance. Erin sauntered towards the bridge, and she lied flat on her stomach with her chin brushing the ground.

I watched her eyes scan the bridge, and I wondered what she was doing.

I was just about to ask when And piped up, "What exactly are you doing?"

"I think it might just be my imagination," she began, "But I think that the boards where the fire shoots out from are reflective. They're as clear as water."

And and I both rose to our feet, and we lay down next to her. It took a few moments for my eyes to adjust, but after a few minutes I could tell that she was right. The fire boards had a glossy substance covering them. It made them appear to be shiny and reflective.

"I can see it!" I exclaimed.

"Well, I guess our problem is solved then," Erin declared.

"Ummm, how?" And questioned.

"We can have one person watching the boards. Then, someone else can start walking across. If they get close to a hot spot, the person who is watching can tell them where to go. Then, we won't have to worry about becoming a pile of ashes," Erin explained.

"Oh," And groaned, "now I feel like a complete idiot."

"It's okay," Erin stated, "I think that all the time."

"Think what?" he asked.

"That you're a complete idiot," she teased.

"Oh, that's it," And insisted, "Next time I am throwing you off the bridge," he chuckled, and small wrinkles formed around the corners of his eyes.

Erin scrambled to her feet and shook her head, "You know, if it weren't for me, we wouldn't have gotten through a lot of the things we've faced," she reminded him.

"Fair enough," And laughed, "So, uh, which one of us is going to go first?"

"Not me," I put my hands out in front of me and started walking backwards.

"Me neither," And proclaimed, "You had the idea, so why don't you go first?" he pointed at Erin and nudged her towards the bridge.

"Well, look who isn't the hero anymore," she eyed And, "Just don't let me die."

"That's not my problem," And teased. Erin paused and took a few deep breaths. She rolled her shoulders back and started stalking across the bridge. It wasn't long before she reached her first fire board.

"Stop!" I called. She froze and waited for her next direction. She had one foot in the air, but she didn't dare move a muscle.

"Take three small steps to the left," And told her. She did as she was told, and she stopped again.

"Can I go straight now?" she asked.

"Yes, but no more than like ten feet. After that, stop again," I commanded.

She gave a thumbs up, "Got it." As she walked she counted her steps on her fingers. She was constantly biting the corner of her lip and looking towards the ceiling. I didn't know if she was praying, or if she was just calculating the distance she had walked.

Using this method was fairly efficient. Erin made it

across after fifteen or twenty minutes, and I went next. It took me longer because I had to look down at my hands whenever they told me to go left or right. However, it was easier because I had people watching from both directions. It made me feel safe (well, as safe as a person could feel given the situation).

Lastly it was And's turn. He walked straight, and then we called out for him to stop. He stopped. He put his life in our hands, and we made a mistake. It was simple, but our room for error was nonexistent.

We forgot he was facing the other way from us. He thought we wanted him to go to his right. We wanted him to go to ours. He ended up right on top of a fire board. A spark appeared in the center of the board.

"Move back!" Erin screeched. He jumped back, but not fast enough. The board went up in flames and while doing so it caught the front of his shirt on fire.

He desperately tried to put it out. He rolled his shirt into a ball and tried to suffocate the flame, but it didn't work. The fire only spread. It couldn't be contained. Erin rose to her feet to go help him, but I pulled her back down. There was nothing she could do to help.

She glared at me, but luckily she listened. When we looked back at And I knew I had made the right call. He had managed to pull his shirt off. It now lay back on the platform. It was far enough away that it didn't pose an immediate threat. A feeling inside of me longed to get out of there as soon as possible, I didn't like the position we were in. It didn't feel right.

He now stood waiting for directions. He looked

like he was ready to question everything we told him. I couldn't blame him. I would have felt the exact same way if it had been me standing out there.

"Take two steps to our right!" I yelled. I made sure to be specific with every direction I gave. There was no way I would let him get hurt for my mistakes again.

Eventually he made it. He took the most time by far. He was constantly hesitating, and stopping to capture his focus. When he reached us he was still in shock. Erin threw her arms around him. He tensed up at first, but after a moment he relaxed. That hug was gravity, and it pulled him back to Earth.

"Thank God you're okay!" she exclaimed through tears of joy, "Do you need any water or bandages?"

"I am fine," he responded. His lips were resting on the top of her head, and it muffled his voice. After a moment they both let go and turned to me.

"So, uh, what do we do now?" I asked. I felt awkward being there. It was like I was trespassing on private property, and I didn't belong.

"We keep walking until we get to the next obstacle. When we do, we'll figure out a way to pass it without being killed," And suggested.

"Sounds like a smart plan. I especially enjoy the part that involves not dying," I agreed.

CHAPTER V
ERIN

For the first time I regretted entering the maze. What would things be like if I had stayed in Millennia? Did And and Alex hate me for coming up with such a stupid plan? They didn't have the option to turn back anymore. If anything happened it would be my fault.

Half of the bridge was broken and it could not be repaired. I was trapped, and there was no one I could blame for this happening. There was no one to blame but myself.

My legs burned from walking, and my whole body ached. I felt sick to my stomach whenever I thought about the bridges. And had nearly fallen to his death and been burned alive. Alex had a gash in his foot from the dagger, and I was still trembling from my almost fall. Today wasn't a very rewarding day.

I counted my breaths and steps. I'd always done this. It keep my mind from wandering. If I set it free, all I could think of were the bad things I'd done. The pain and danger I had caused then felt like an endless list. I couldn't stomach the thought of what was next.

I had been walking behind And, and Alex was by my side. Suddenly And came to a stop. I hadn't been expecting it, and I almost ran into him. I peered around him to see why we had stopped moving. What I saw made my stomach drop.

A huge cliff loomed over open air. Above it hung a frail looking rope. It ran parallel to the ceiling, and ended on the other side. There, a landing area stood. The size of it was not in our favor (to say the least). There was no other way for us to go. We had walked straight here from the bridge. On the way we didn't pass any detours. I didn't know what to say, so I waited for someone else to speak up.

"Well, this is going to be very interesting. Please tell me that someone has a plan?" Alex looked at And and me with hopeful eyes. Unfortunately, I had been hoping for the same thing. We needed an idea that was creative, but not suicidal. Those however, were not my specialty.

"I think we only have one option," And concluded, "We have to hang from the rope and just keep moving one hand in front of the other. Most importantly, we have to pray we won't slip."

"I don't think there's any other way," I admitted, "So let's quit wasting time and get going."

"Yes, the sooner we can get this over with, the better," And agreed, "Alex or I will go first. You will go next, and one of us will go last."

"How did you come up with that order?" Alex

questioned.

"Because," And acted like it was the most obvious thing in the world, "Erin is too short to reach the rope, she will need help getting up and down."

"Hey! I am not that short; well, at least not for a girl my age," I argued.

"There's no need for you to get all defensive," And reminded me, "And I didn't say you were short. I said that you were too short to reach the rope."

"Whatever," I exhaled, "Will one of you go already then?"

"Gladly," Alex pushed past me. When he lifted his arms, his fingers brushed the bottom of the rope. He had to lean up onto his toes to wrap his hands around it.

He cautiously moved one hand in front of the other. Before I knew it, he was almost there. When he only had a few feet left to go, he swung himself forward. He landed perfectly on the narrow strip of land. He straightened himself and took a bow. I couldn't help but roll my eyes and smile.

Now it was my turn. And lifted me up. When he did, I was as light as cotton. Just as I grabbed onto the rope he whispered in my ear.

"I don't suggest attempting the same finish as Alex. He was being a showoff and could have gotten killed," And chuckled, "don't take offense. I'm not saying you're not capable of doing what he did, I just don't want to see you mess up and get hurt."

I could feel his warm breath against my skin, and it sent tingles through my body. I wondered if he knew my nerves were a result of being so close to him or if he thought I was nervous about the obstacle. Either way, he didn't acknowledge them which made me feel like he was confident in me; like he was confident that I could perform in the presence of fear.

"I hate to break it to you, but I'm not in love with the thought of death. You have nothing to worry about," I giggled.

"Dang it," he joked.

"Hello! Are you going to come or not?" Alex called.

"I'll be right there," I shouted back to him.

"Well, hurry up," he yelled.

"Okay, okay I'm coming. Just have a little patience," I screamed.

"Good luck, and try not to fall," And grinned.

"Thanks, and I promise I'll do my best to hold on," I answered. And let go of my waist, but I could still feel the pressure and warmth of his hands.

Left, right, left, right. My brain wasn't prepared for this. I had to concentrate. If I didn't, all I saw were visions of falling. My arms were shaking. I had to go fast if I wanted to survive. There was no room for hesitation.

I glanced up, and I saw Alex waiting for me. I thought of his spectacular finish. I considered attempting it, but not for long. I knew I would never be able to accomplish it. Falling into blackness and waiting for death didn't sound appealing. Daredevil moves were out of the question.

I only had a few feet left. My fingers were

constantly slipping. My strength wouldn't be enough to overpower gravity soon. I didn't lift my hands anymore; instead I slid them along the rope. If I let go for one moment, it could result in the end of my life.

I was almost there. I was so close to getting there. Then, the sound of fabric tearing began to break out. Its echo bounced between the cliffs' walls. The next few moments after that were a blur. The rope snapped, and I flew forward.

Luckily, Alex broke my fall. Both of us fell to the ground. We scrambled to our feet, and looked across the gap towards And. He was still on the other side, and there was no way for him to cross now. This was going to require a lot of resourcefulness.

"Well, the landing wasn't quite as graceful as Alex's," And snickered, "but I would rate it a solid eight out of ten."

"Not that I don't love listening to you discuss my greatness," I began, "but how exactly do you plan on crossing the pit now?"

"I have absolutely no idea," And said, "but I am certain that I will come up with something incredible. Who knew having pure skill and immense knowledge would come in handy this often." His voice imitated an arrogant, rich kid.

"Sure you will, and it will be something completely incredible," I mocked him.

"Yes, thank you so much for your support," he replied.

Alex and I sat and waited for And to figure out his

"incredible plan." It felt like forever, but at last And spoke up.

"My incredible plan is checked out of the library at the moment. And the Library of And's Mind is very exclusive, so there is only one copy of each thought. Therefore, I have decided to be open to your ideas," he announced.

"Why don't you just swing on the rope from your end? Then, you can grab onto the other rope. After that, you could swing forward and drop when you are above the platform," Alex suggested.

"How long have you been thinking about that?" I asked him.

"The past few hours," he answered. I elbowed him in the side.

"What was that for?" he demanded.

"That was for not speaking up sooner. Do you know how much time we spent waiting around when you had a perfect plan? That is, if And is capable of what you suggested," I blurted.

"I didn't say it because I thought it was stupid," he argued, "I was also curious if genius would be able to come up with something. After all, he does have 'pure skill and immense knowledge.'"

"Don't mock me," And warned, "And yes, I am quite capable of accomplishing that plan. As a matter of fact, it will be a piece of cake."

"If it's going to be so easy, then why aren't you here yet? If it was that easy, you would have at least started by now. Why don't you just go already? I'm getting tired of waiting," I challenged.

"Whatever you want, your majesty," he leaned forward and snatched the rope out of the air.

A second later he jumped, and now he was soaring through the air. He reached out in front of him, and he just missed the second rope. He swung back, and nearly smacked into the wall on the other side.

This time, when he swung back towards the rope it was much more powerful. He released the first rope, and reached for the second one. He missed it. He started to fall. As much as I wanted to look away, I couldn't. I was frozen in place.

He was desperately trying to grab hold of either rope. Finally, he caught the second one. He caught it inches away from the end. If he tried to swing over to the ledge now, he would hit the jagged edge.

He grunted as he heaved himself up. He had to climb up a few feet (at least), before it would be safe for him to swing. His muscles were visible through his shirt as he was climbing.

I quickly looked away. I was embarrassed for having stared at him. At least he had put on his spare shirt while we were walking. I could still see his perfect abs in my mind. His six pack looked like it had been carved by a master artist. It was random; but it was one of those things you know will stay in your mind for the rest of your life.

Alex pulled me to the side of the cliff as And began to swing towards the ledge. He was like an eagle gliding through the air. It made me feel self-conscious. I was the only one who didn't have a glamorous landing.

When And landed on the ledge, the sound of thunder filled the air. It surprised me, and I nearly fell. If there wasn't a wall behind me, I probably would have. And took a few seconds to regain his balance, and then he trotted over to Alex and me.

"Nice landing," I commented.

"I was as graceful as a swan," And insisted. He leaned forward onto one foot, imitating a swan.

"I wouldn't suggest doing that if you ever come across a swan," I informed him, "you might offend it."

"I don't think I could ever offend a swan, I am too pretty," he argued. I couldn't help but laugh.

"Sure..," I said, "I'll agree with you if we can find a place to rest now. I for one am totally exhausted."

"You're not the one who had to do a circus act," And suggested, "Why don't we just set up right here? It's a good place. The cliff blocks us from any danger on the side which will make it easy to keep watch."

"Works for me," I agreed. We didn't even bother setting up camp that night. We just fell asleep using our backpacks as pillows.

I fell asleep the second my back touched the ground. I slept the entire time I wasn't on watch, and by the morning I was fully rested. I was ready to conquer whatever was going to come next.

Later that day, I was even more grateful to be fully rested. The first obstacle we had to pass was a set of monkey bars. And and Alex had both grown up with them around, so they crossed them with no problem.

I on the other hand, was not so flawless. My hands

kept getting sweaty, and I was constantly slipping. At one point, I had to hold onto the bar with my feet because I needed to wipe my hands on my pants.

The quality of the bars was not in my favor either. They were so rusty, they didn't even swing. Again, this was no problem for And and Alex. However, my arms were too short. I couldn't reach the next bar if the one I was on didn't move.

And and Alex had to go across the bars multiple times, even then they never fully loosened; but at this point, the bars could swing. I still didn't like it because when they did, they made an ear shattering creak that made all of us cringe.

By the time I had finally made it across the bars, I was exhausted. Hours of time had been lost, and it wasn't even something we needed to think about. The next obstacle was much easier. There was a steel cable. It ran from one cliff to another.

It was very similar to the rope because it ran between two ledges. This one was much longer. On the other side, there was a contraption they were certain we could use to get across. I doubted them, but I went along with it anyway.

And and Alex referred to this obstacle as a "zip line." They explained why we couldn't hold onto the cable. If we tried, it would cut our hands. Then we would become distracted, and ultimately we would end up falling.

This meant that we had to reach the contraption on the other side. We spent hours discussing and arguing about ideas. In the end it was decided we would tie the ropes together, and Alex would lasso the contraption. Then we could pull it to the other side.

It ended up being easier said than done. Alex took forever to catch the contraption. Once he did, he moved too quickly. We had to completely start over. Luckily we were able to get it completely across on the second try.

The contraption was three wheels connected together by a metal wire. There were two carabineers attached to the wire. One of them held the wheels to the cable. Meanwhile, the other attached a silver horseshoe-shaped pole to the wheels.

And went first, and he propelled through the air like a majestic bird. He landed swiftly on his feet, and flung the contraption back to the other ledge. It only made it about halfway, so Alex had to lasso it again. This time he was quicker at retrieving it, but it still took him a few tries. I was starting to become bored.

When he finally got it, he told me to take a running start. I needed to make myself as aerodynamic as possible. I did as I was told, but I was only able to move for a few seconds before I came to a complete stop.

I was suspended above the middle of the pit. I was right between the two ledges, and I was as far from one as I was from the other. I could tell And and Alex hadn't been considering the possibility of this. They both stood watching me with blank faces. I didn't think either of them knew what to do.

"Um, what exactly am I supposed to do now?" I asked. They continued to stare for a few moments before I finally got an answer.

"Is there any way that you can make it go any further?" Alex asked.

"If there was, do you think I would still be hanging here?" I snapped.

"Well, sorry," he said sarcastically. I hadn't meant to be mean, but when I was frightened my words tended to come across that way.

"Any other ideas?" I asked hopefully.

"Not at the moment," he answered. His voice was calmer; he had finally realized I was scared and stressed out.

"Oh," I said, "I have a feeling this isn't going to turn out well..,"

I felt uneasy hanging there because I knew I could fall to my death at any moment. My hands were shaking, and I began to wonder how much longer I would be able to hold on. I didn't think it would be much longer.

My fingertips started to slide downward, and my anxiety started to grow. I held onto the bar as tightly as I could. I could feel my fingernails digging into the top of my thumb. All I could do was hold on and wait. I really hated not being in control of my own life right now.

"Can you lift your feet up high enough to reach the cable?" And's voice echoed off the hard stone walls.

"I think so," I guessed, "Why?"

"If your feet can touch the cable, you can pull yourself across to the ledge," he explained.

At last we had a solution. When I lifted my feet they brushed the cable. It took a while before I could get across because my legs became tired very quickly.

Therefore, I could only move a few inches at a time.

I finally reached the other side, and my arms felt like they were going to fall off. My legs and stomach muscles ached, and my lungs were burning. I didn't expect it to be very hard, but I felt like I had just climbed Everest.

"I have to admit, I wasn't sure if you would be able to get across like that," And commented.

"Well, I didn't really have a choice," I replied, "the only other option I had was waiting for my hands to slip and hoping that my death wouldn't be painful. Obviously that was not a favorable option."

"Good enough," And leaned across me and grabbed onto the handle. He wrapped his hand against my waist and held me against his chest to keep me from falling. The aches and pains in my stomach turned into butterflies. This time he was able to fling it all the way back to the other side, and Alex didn't have to lasso it again.

Alex shoved the ropes into his backpack. He looked pleased because he didn't have to lasso anything this time. He grabbed onto the handle, and he pulled it back until it was at the beginning of the cable.

He took a running start and leaped off of the platform. He was a blur in the air, and I was startled when he appeared next to me so suddenly.

"Very nice," I applauded.
"Oh, thank you. You know it is my specialty," he joked. I nodded and laughed.

I enjoyed being around And and Alex. I didn't have a brother, but they had begun to feel like older siblings to me. It was fun teasing each other. Annie had never liked being teased, so I had to refrain from it. I didn't realize how much fun it was to joke around and be sarcastic until now.

"It might be a specialty for you, but it is far from one of Erin's," And snickered.

"I prefer to specialize in more important things," I claimed.

"I guess we will see about that," And contradicted.

This time when we were walking it felt more comfortable. We were all chatting and taunting each other. When we approached the next obstacle, my heart stopped. I frantically looked back down the long tunnel we had been walking through; hopefully there was another route we could take.

Standing before us was a vast sheet of black. The only way to get across it was by jumping from one platform to another. The number of platforms was endless; but all of them were no bigger than two square feet, and they were placed several feet apart.

I knew I could jump fairly far, but I'd always had a running start, and something to catch me if I fell. Here I didn't have either of these things, and to be honest it terrified me.

The area we had to cover was so huge; I couldn't even see the end of it. I was certain it would take me the rest of the day just to get across half of it.

And went first. The gap between us and the first platform was the only one I knew I could pass. And did it with no trouble, and when he reached the platform he started to bounce.

"The platforms are trampolines!" he exclaimed.

"Awesome!" Alex called. I just stood there confused, and waited for one of them to explain what a trampoline was.

"Is everything good Erin?" And asked, "You don't seem very excited."

"Yeah it's fine; I just don't exactly know what a trampoline is..," I trailed off.

"Well, I guess you are going to find out," And sounded amused, "Here, jump to where I am."

"Okay," I agreed. I took a deep breath, and then I ran and jumped. I didn't open my eyes until I stopped moving.

And had caught me, and when my eyes were fully opened he set me down. The floor below me went downward and my eyes widened. I opened my mouth to ask if the trampoline was going to break, but before I could ask And spoke up.

"Jump. You will be surprised what happens," he said. He took my hands, and we both jumped. When we jumped, the bottom of the trampoline sprang upward. We went flying into the air, and I shrieked with joy.

"Now do you feel more confident about getting from platform to platform?" he asked.

"Definitely," I couldn't believe we didn't have these trampoline things back home. They were so much fun. I felt like I was flying through the air whenever I jumped. It was one of the best feelings in the world.

And and I crossed the blackness together because I wasn't completely familiar with trampolines. Although they were fun, it was hard to keep your balance. The whole experience was absolutely nerve wracking.

Alex was right behind us because the trampolines weren't big enough to hold all three of us. He seemed to be enjoying himself because he kept hollering out in joy. I felt like doing the same, but I was too nervous to try it. I thought it would distract me, and make me fall.

Soon we were in the middle of the darkness. I could just barely make out the outlines of where we began. Our finishing point was becoming clearer and clearer. Part of me was excited. The rest of me wanted this to last forever.

I couldn't believe it. I didn't think I was ever going to enjoy an obstacle. They usually made me miserable, and stressed me out. I felt so happy at that moment, and I knew I would never forget it. And and I were still holding hands, and we skipped from one platform to the next without stopping.

When we reached the other side I was probably smiling like an idiot, but I didn't care. And's smile was genuine, and it never wavered. It was confident and happy. When Alex reached us, And casually dropped my hand. I was expecting it, but I couldn't help feeling a little disappointed.

"How was your first trampoline experience?" Alex grinned.

"It was fabulous," I replied, "I don't know why we don't have them above the ground."

"Well, I am glad that And and I were ones who got to introduce you to them," Alex noted.

"Me, too," I confirmed, "They seemed to come just

in time. That was actually fun. I can't believe it was a roadblock, especially after facing the others."

"It was probably meant to intimidate us, and if you weren't careful, you could have fallen off," And pointed out.

"I guess so," I answered, "Do you think we'll have more things like this?"

"I would think no. If we passed the first one, it means we could pass it again. From what I know about the maze, it was constructed to be difficult for everyone. Some of the obstacles will be easy for us, and some will seem impossible. For other people it could be entirely different. And nothing is repeated in order to be as challenging as possible," And seemed just as disappointed as I felt.

"How did you learn so much about the maze?" I questioned.

And replied, "In school, one week of every month was set aside to study the maze. We were lectured about the history and creation of it. We also learned about what some of the obstacles are, and what they are intended to do. Mostly the teachers talked about how dangerous it is, and they warned us to stay away from it."

"What specifically did you learn about it?" I asked.

"Well, you have already heard the history. So I am guessing that means you are asking about the obstacles, right?" he guessed.

"Yeah," I responded.

"We learned that they were dangerous, but there was a way to pass every one of them. You just have to be patient and not rush into it. The exact number of obstacles is unknown, but we think there are a ton of them; however, we will most likely not have to get past them all. The maze is in the shape of a huge square. In the center, there is a large open space. This is the only known entrance in existence. Every route from Millennia to the center has at least one type of obstacle. Most of them are meant to kill or injure the traveler enough that they will give up. The next most common ones are brain teasers. They are meant to slow people down significantly, and sometimes drive them insane. The third type is like what we just passed. These are used to intimidate people, but there are very few of them because they usually never work," he explained.

"Wow, that must have taken forever to memorize," I was amazed until a slight anger crept into my mind, so I continued by saying, "wait a minute, why didn't you tell me all of this sooner? You had no right to keep me in the dark like that. I should have been informed about all of this before I set foot in the maze. What's wrong with you!"

"It's common knowledge, so I guess I assumed that you would have already known. You could ask almost anyone about it and they would be able to tell you. Once you learn it, you never forget it," he responded.

Anger still existed inside of me; but I didn't know how to respond, and I felt guilty for accusing him the way I did, so I didn't say anything more. We turned to keep going, and a giant arch loomed before us. The top was lined with symbols, and the sides were covered in small, intricate details. I tried to decipher the symbols on my own, but I gave up when Alex started to read them.

"Here lies the Creature Chambers. Beware or hope

you are lucky," he added, "It's in the first language which was created by the founders of Millennia. It is hardly ever used, except for signatures. We primarily use other languages that were created before life underground, like English and French, but the first language is sacred. Every citizen in Millennia is required to know it."

"I don't suppose either of you know what the Creature Chambers are, do you?" I wondered.

" I have no idea," And answered, "but I think that we are about to find out."

CHAPTER VI
ALEX

Once we had passed the trampolines, I knew whatever came next was not going to be as easy. The Creature Chambers was something I had never heard of. I imagined what would happen when we walked in. We would probably be attacked by deadly animals trying to kill us. I really hoped I was wrong.

Meanwhile, And and Erin were starting to get on my nerves. Half the time they didn't even acknowledge the fact that I existed, and whenever they did it was because I was almost dead or they needed something from me. I was the angriest I had been at And for coming into the maze with us.

We approached the doors that lead to the Creature Chambers. They rose to the ceiling, and they covered most of the wall which had originally been there. The doors were made of dark brown wood, and they had handles in the shape of a lion's head that were made of brass.

It took all three of us to pull open the door because it was so heavy. When we pulled it open, it shrieked, and I instinctively reached for my knife. When nothing happened I began to worry.

If the Creature Chambers were empty, the cannibals could be close. If they were able to kill all of the creatures, we had definitely been underestimating them. I saw a movement in the corner of my eye, and I instantly knew creatures still inhabited the chambers.

A large black pair of wings came towards me, and I had to drop to the floor to avoid them. When I looked up, I saw we were surrounded by none other than a swarm of killer ravens. I thought about running, but I knew I would never make it to the door in time.

The killer ravens were strong and fast. They were no match for a mere human. Smooth, black feathers with sharp points on the end covered their bodies. They had red eyes that were both shrewd and bloodthirsty. Pairs of eyes were all I could see when their bodies melted into the shadows. Their gleaming, golden beaks were sharp and knife-like.

In total I could see fourteen of them. Good fighters might be able to handle one or two, but not even the best could last more than a few minutes against this many. Fighting them was not going to be our smartest option. It was barely an option at all.

In the corner was a pile of bones. When I looked more closely I recognized them. They were human bones. Blood smeared the floor, and in another corner there was a second pile of bones, but these bones weren't human. They were killer raven.

There was no sign of food anywhere. They had been feeding on each other in order to survive. Their species has been commonly known to resort to cannibalism in times of need. They were probably eager to eat something other than their own kind, so I wondered why they hadn't attacked yet. I turned to And who sat on the floor digging through his pack.

"What are you doing?" I hissed. I tried not to draw any attention to myself because as soon as I did the birds were probably going to attack.

"I am looking for something to eat," he replied.

"This is not the time to be snacking," I snapped, "If you haven't noticed, we are surrounded by killer ravens."

"I am quite aware of that. Just in case you forgot, I am not an idiot," he responded,

"The snack isn't for me. It's to lure the birds away from the door so we can make a break for it. If we're lucky, we might be able to make it with a little time to spare."

"Oh," was all I said. I felt foolish for thinking And would do something so careless and absurd, but I felt even more stupid for not thinking of it sooner.

"I found some," Erin spoke up. Unlike me, she had caught onto his plan and was helping him search.

"Thank God," And said, "I thought we had run out of food already. Toss it to me."

Erin tossed the food to And. It was a bag full of dried meat. He took a handful out and put the rest of it into his backpack. The second he opened the bag all of the birds began to gather around him.

He threw the meat into the corner furthest from us and the door, and we darted to the exit. The birds were fighting over the food, but as soon as it was gone they turned their attention back to us.

The first bird reached us just as we were opening the door. We leaped into the next room and slammed the door behind us, but it wouldn't close. At least half of the birds had stuck their heads or a wing into the space between the door and the wall.

The space wasn't large enough for them to get through, but if we stopped trying to close the door, the birds would burst through and eat us. In total, seven of the birds had managed to get in the space.

Before I could think of anything to do And had already started to save the day, again.

He kept his back pushing the door closed, but he had carefully inched his way to the edge of the door. He stabbed the birds that were in the way one by one with the tip of his knife.

When they were stabbed they cried out in pain. It distracted them, and they moved away from the door. By the time And had stabbed all of the birds, the door slid shut and clicked into place. On the other side of the door there were lots of loud noises. It sounded like they were trying to break down the door. This would have worried me if I hadn't noticed what was in the second chamber.

At the far end of the chamber there was a line of eight poison penguins. These were some of the most deadly creatures known to Millennia. This was because they were very easy to confuse with normal penguins which were cute and cuddly.

Poison penguins were as far as you could get from cute and cuddly. If any part of your skin touched them, it would feel like a thick, sharp, boiling hot needle was being plunged into your skin. Next thing you know, that portion of your skin would have dissolved.

However, that was not what gave them their name. Their bite was as poisonous as you can get. If one of them bit you, it meant you had seven seconds left to live. No amount of medical help or medication can change that.

Right now, they were faced towards the door. This meant they hadn't noticed us yet, and we still had time to think of a plan. I saw something move to the side of me, and when I turned I recognized Erin's silhouette.

I wanted to ask her what exactly she was doing, but I couldn't. If we made one sound the penguins would turn around, and we would be dead in a matter of moments. I watched where she was going, and then she stopped.

She was in the middle of the room, and she was leaning against the wall. She motioned for And and I to come, so we did. We were not as silent as she had been, but luckily the penguins hadn't turned around.

I wondered if they were deaf. They hadn't turned around when the birds were pounding against the door, and they hadn't noticed any of us moving. After a few moments of walking as quietly as I could, I gave up.

Walking quietly meant I was going slowly. And had almost reached Erin, and I wasn't even close. I knew it was stupid to take chances, but my common sense had been replaced by my ego.

I jogged to catch up with them, and when I was only a few steps away my knife fell from the pouch on my belt loop and clattered to the floor. A sharp sound rang through the air, and one by one the penguins turned around.

Their eyes focused directly on me, and they rushed towards me like a bullet. And and Erin started going up, and then I realized they had been standing by a ladder. It creaked with every step they took, but still the penguins advanced towards me.

I scooped up my knife from the floor and sprinted towards the ladder. I slipped one of the ropes from my backpack. I thought I could toss it up to And and Erin once I got there. Then they could help me up before I became dead meat, literally. That ended up not being what I used it for at all.

A penguin was standing in front of the ladder when I got there. It crouched down like it was going to lunge at me. I swung the rope towards it, and it met the bird square in the jaw. It growled at me and lunged again.

This time I hit it in the side. The rope slid across the bird's feathers, and knocked it out of my way. The second the rope was no longer touching the penguin, it burst into flames because of the friction.

I scrambled to get a hold of the ladder, and started to climb. My hands were sweating, and my feet kept slipping. And and Erin had already climbed up the ladder, and now they were climbing across the ceiling which was covered in bars.

They formed a pattern of squares, and at the door

there was a long, slender bar they could slide down on. They would land on the arch of the next door. It was a perfect escape route.

I had climbed the first ten bars or so, when I heard a snap below me. The bar my feet had been on fell from the ladder. I looked down to see what had happened. The penguins were tossing each other up in an attempt to reach me. I was lucky, only the bar had been broken this time. Next time I was probably going to be bitten.

This motivated me to move even faster. Soon I had gotten twice as far as I had been before, and it had only taken half the time. The penguins had broken three bars so far, but I had been able to move to the next before it broke each time.

Before I knew it, I was climbing along the ceiling. And and Erin were sitting on the arch of the second door, waiting for me. The ceiling was much harder to climb across because I had to hold on using only my arms.

All of a sudden, a penguin shot up out of nowhere into the air. It grabbed onto my shoe with its beak. I kicked at it, but it wouldn't let go. I kept moving, but it was weighing me down, and I was about to fall. I ended up having to slide my shoe off to avoid falling. Soon after, another penguin flew up into the air.

It would have grabbed onto my other shoe or bitten my foot if I hadn't flung my feet up into the bars. It came up short from reaching me, as did all of the other penguins that were tossed up after that.

With my feet on the bars I was able to move much faster than before, and I reached Erin and And in a matter of seconds. When I slid down the pole onto the arch, And and Erin slid mostly off of the arch; now they were holding on by only their hands.

They kicked the door over and over again until it finally flew open. There was a ladder on the back of the next door, and we grabbed hold of it as we fell from the arch. We didn't even bother with climbing down it. Instead, we slid down it as if it were a fire pole. The door shut just before the penguins reached it.

The second my feet touched the ground I saw clawed rabbits racing towards us. This time there was no place to run. Our only option was to fight them. Their mouths were foaming, and their rib cages were showing. They were ready for a meal.

"Get your knives ready," And instructed. Erin swiftly slid the knife from its holder, and into the palm of her hand. I on the other hand was much clumsier. My hands shook, and I struggled to stop the knife from falling out of my hand.

When the rabbits reached us, they immediately started clawing at our feet and ankles. Soon my pants became shredded, and they were stained with blood. I slashed out at the rabbit, but it dodged the knife. I hadn't even come close to hitting it.

It growled and started clawing at me again. Its mouth was still foaming, and my sock was starting to feel wet and sticky. I kept swinging my knife, hoping to connect at least once. The rabbit dodged every blow with expert agility.

I moved backwards until my back was against the

wall. In total, there were only six of them; however, there appeared to be many more. They moved so quickly that they were only blurs. They were a million places at once.

I hadn't heard a sound from And and Erin. When I turned towards them, they were fighting side by side. They were on their knees, and their backs were pressed against the wall. There was a dead rabbit lying a few feet away from them. A few of the others had blood- stained fur. Some of them were even missing chunks of flesh.

The rabbit who had been attacking me took this as an opportunity. I had lost focus. It had only been for a moment, but that moment was significant. The rabbit lunged towards my face with his claws out in front of him. His claws sank into my face, and his mouth was opened wide and ready to bite me.

The bite of a clawed rabbit wouldn't kill you (like a poison penguin), but it was much more painful. Even after the rabbit had unclenched its teeth you could still feel it. A thick, black scar was left behind, and it oozed a tar-like liquid.

I lifted my arm, and for the first time I connected. I stabbed it in the back, and instantly it let go of my face and fell to the ground. Blood was dripping down my face into the corners of my eyes and mouth, and the rabbit was coughing up blood.

I knew I had to kill it before it attacked me again, but I couldn't bring myself to do it until I told myself it was in pain. I was doing it a favor by killing it; then it wouldn't have to suffer. Its spine had most likely been broken, and it would be paralyzed if it didn't bleed to death.

I thrust the blade of my knife towards the rabbit's heart, and I heard a soft whimper which was soon replaced by silence. I looked down and saw the body of the rabbit, still and unmoving. I knew it tried to kill me first, but I couldn't help feeling guilty.

A pool of blood was surrounding it, and its eyes were glass marbles. I wanted to turn away, but I couldn't. I just stood there, thinking about what I had done. It wasn't long before another rabbit came towards me. I felt like a bloodthirsty monster that would rather kill than die.

My brain zeroed in on the new threat, and I was grateful for the distraction. If it hadn't come, I might still be there wondering what turned me into a murderer. This rabbit was not as swift as the other had been, and I assumed the deep cut in its left back leg had something to do with it.

Its lack of speed allowed me to glance towards And and Erin. Their progress was spectacular. Three dead rabbits were lying by their feet, and they were fighting the last one (apart from the one I was currently fighting).

The rabbit they were fighting seemed to be the most skilled of them all. Even with both of them fighting, it was clear they were the underdogs. Their arms were covered with jagged cuts and scratches, and their hands and knives were coated in blood.

Like mine, the bottom of their pants were shredded and stained with blood. I turned away when the rabbit sank its teeth into Erin's palm. She screamed in pain and stabbed the rabbit in the shoulder. In the brief pause (when it let go and started falling) And plunged the blade into the rabbit's neck, and it instantly went limp. It fell off the blade and landed on the floor with one eye open.

I turned to finish the rabbit I was fighting, and I swung my blade towards it. It was able to dodge my first few attempts, but then I hit it in the side. It fell onto its back and curled into a ball on the floor. It was unable to get up, so it just slashed at me with its claws. This time when I killed it, I turned away and didn't look back.

I rushed to And and Erin to make sure she was alright from the bite. When I reached them, And was wrapping her hand in a strip of cloth he'd cut from the bottom of his shirt. It was immediately soaked with her blood. Erin was squeezing his forearm in an attempt to get her mind away from the pain, and when she let go a faint handprint was left behind.

And finished quickly and turned towards me, "You look terrible."

"And you look like model material right now," I scoffed.

"Actually I think I do," he posed, "I could be on one of those magazine advertisements for skateboards, or leather jackets, or something." Erin and I burst out laughing.

She patted him on the shoulder with her good hand, "Think what you want to..,"

"Don't worry, I always do that," he grinned, "Sit down, Alex, then I can make it so that your face doesn't get infected."

I sat, and And produced a small round container from a pocket in his bag. When he unscrewed it, I didn't recognize what was inside. It was a foggy, thick, creamy liquid. He put a thin layer along my face.

I thought I was being attacked by a swarm of bees. After a few seconds the pain was gone, and the weird liquid had hardened on my face. I would have asked what it was, but it was so strong and sticky, I couldn't move my face.

"It's the blood from a rare snake called Slithering Silver. The snake's bite is deadly, but its blood can heal almost any wound," he read my mind, "Anyway, your face should be back to normal in about an hour or so."

"Why didn't we use that before?" Erin asked.

"It will only work on a wound that was inflicted by an animal," he explained.

"Okay," Erin seemed curious, but she was satisfied with the response, "Are you two ready to open the next door?"

"I don't think we'll ever be ready," And responded, "but I think we should try to get this over with as soon as possible."

We walked along the room to the next door. I wondered how many more of these doors we would have to go through. Hopefully we had made it past the Creature Chambers, but it could go on forever. The only relieving thing about opening this door was we could come back into this room if we got overwhelmed or needed to regroup.

This door was red-brown in color, and the handle was a thick, black disk. We turned it, and it moved smoothly. The door swung straight open. There was what looked like long, glass display cases covering every wall.

I couldn't get a very good view of the room because my eyes were stuck half shut and half open from the snake blood And put on my face. I felt a sting on my arm, and the next thing I knew And and Erin were pulling me back into the room. They slammed the door shut and locked it behind us.

"I think Alex was bitten," And panicked, "Are you alright, Erin?"

"Yeah," she replied, "I'm just, you know, a little freaked out. What exactly were those things? I haven't seen them before."

"Vampire ladybugs," he answered, "They are a manmade breed. At first they were created to be used as weapons against the cannibals, but they ended up being hidden in the maze once it was constructed. I would have told you and Alex before, but I thought they were only rumors, and when I asked teachers they confirmed my theory."

"Just to make sure, there aren't any other "rumors" you want to share with the rest of us?" she sounded angry because she hadn't been told.

"Not off the top of my head, but I will tell you if I think of any," he promised, "right now, we need to take care of Alex, he was definitely bitten."

"What happens if you are bitten by one of them?" she quavered.

"If it is a small bite, nothing happens. However, if the bug starts to feed off of you, then you will be infected by its venom. Even though it only feels like a bee sting, it temporarily paralyzes you. At first you are aware of what is going on, but after a few minutes, the venom starts to spread. When it spreads, it sends waves of energy through your body. The energy makes you feel happy, but before you know it, you are dead."

"Is Alex going to be okay?" Erin worried.

"He should be. We pulled him away before too much of the venom was released into his system. What worries me is how we're going to get past the bugs."

"At least we know what we're up against now," Erin said. I didn't hear the rest of the conversation. My eyes shut and they refused to open. I had drifted into a deep sleep without even realizing it.

When I woke up And and Erin told me what had happened. They told me they had to cut my arm so the venom could bleed out. My arm would be sore, but I should be just fine. The stuff on my face was no longer hard, and in its place was smooth new skin.

They wasted no time and started explaining the plan. First, we needed to cover ourselves in blankets (this would help keep us from being bitten). Then we would go into one of the long, glass display cases.

We would close them behind us and walk to the other side of the door. After that we would come out of the cases and go into the next room as soon as possible.

In the end, the plan worked perfectly. None of us were bitten. The bugs didn't even know what was going on until we were in the display cases.

They rammed into the cases over and over again until the outside walls were splattered with them. When we finally reached the end of the case, only a few of them were still alive. We easily opened the door and slipped into the next room unharmed.

The next room was completely filled. Everywhere you looked there were enormous groups of fligerites. Fligerites are a cross breed. They are forty-five percent fly, thirty-five percent bee, and twenty percent tiger.

Not counting their wingspan they are about the size of your fist. They have a single wing that goes over the top of their body (it is about the size of your forearm). They have the eyes, wings, and body type of a fly, the stinger of a bee, and the coloring of a tiger.

Their sting causes immense pain, but humans and large animals aren't affected in any other way. Smaller animals are paralyzed and later eaten.

The reason the fligerites were thriving so well was because there was a large number of them. They are known to become cannibals in times of need.

I hoped they were well fed and would leave us alone. Fligerites weren't the most intelligent animals, but they knew when something was too large for them to kill. They generally left it alone then, but that was not always the case.

We stood still and waited to see if the fligerites would try to kill us. They didn't seem to pay attention to us, so we started to move to the other side of the room. At that point our luck vanished.

We had barely moved away from the wall when fligerites came rushing in our direction. I felt sting after sting, and I waved my arms around like an idiot. My only priority was getting them away from me.

And yelled to keep running. We needed to make it to the other side of the room. I tried to do what he said, but my legs felt like jelly. I fell to my knees, and had to crawl across the floor. And was struggling to get to the other side too, and I had no idea where Erin was.

I spun around a few times before I finally saw her. Her strategy made me feel insanely stupid. She kept her back against the wall. This gave the fligerites a smaller area they could sting, and it was easier for her to focus.

She would take three or four steps towards the wall before stopping to pull the stingers out of her skin. There was no evidence she had ever been stung because she removed the stingers before they could leave any marks.

When I looked back up, And had reached the other side of the room. He was standing in a corner pulling the stingers out of his skin. His skin had turned bright red, and some of the stingers had begun to turn the skin around them purple.

I glanced down at my skin. It was red and blotchy. A chill went down my spine and spread to my fingertips. I knew a few stings wouldn't do any harm, but I had no idea what hundreds would do. Luckily, fligerites only had one stinger. Once it was gone, it was gone forever.

When I looked around, most of the fligerites had lost their stingers. Now they were observing from the opposite side of the room. Even then, nearly a thousand of them still remained. They did not look like they were ready to give up.

I had now reached the center of the room. That was where most remaining fligerites were. They all stung me, and I was overwhelmed in pain. I decided it was time for me to start pulling the stingers out.

When I pulled them out of my skin there was a sharp pinch, and it pulled on my skin. My only choice was to ignore the pain and keep going. Each stinger hurt worse than the last. I was still being stung over and over again, and it seemed like every time I pulled out a stinger five more replaced it.

Finally, the stinging stopped. I quickened my pace, and before I knew it there was a huge pile of stingers in front of me. There had to be at least a hundred of them. I had gotten them out of the front half of my left arm when I saw And rushing over to help me.

He had gotten most of the stingers out of himself, and soon after Erin followed. They both helped me pull the stingers out of my skin. The pain was indescribable. And and Erin were both pulling stingers out two at a time.

I felt numb. I wasn't sure if it was from the pain, or the stingers. Either way I was grateful for it. I ran my hands up and down my arms and felt my rough skin. There were no more stingers on my back and neck, and there were only a few left on my legs.

Erin stopped helping so she could get the stingers out of And's back. In no time at all we were all stinger free. Erin was lucky. She didn't get any stingers in her back, and the others she had pulled out fast enough. Nothing painful happened to her.

And and I, on the other hand were aching. My muscles burned whenever I moved, and I couldn't stretch my arms fully out. I was a concrete sculpture, and I could barely move.

The fligerites were all trying to stay as far away

from us as possible. I had to resist the urge to go kill them all. I probably would have if And and Erin hadn't dragged me across towards the door.

"Come on," Erin spoke softly, "I know you're not in the best possible condition...but we need to keep moving." I knew she was right. I stopped trying to get them to release me, and I relaxed.

"What could possibly be next," I groaned.

"No idea," Erin and And said at the exact same moment.

The last door wasn't much of a door at all. It was a sliding panel. It took all three of us to pull down the lever that opened it, and when we did there was a loud pop. The door started to slide open all on its own.

Pieces of rock and dirt poured out of the top of the opening, and it took a few minutes before the air cleared. I expected to be attacked by some sort of animal, but when nothing happened I looked around; I was trying to find what we were going to battle next.

I stepped forward and the door slid closed behind us. We were standing in a cold, dark room. There was no light, and I couldn't see my hand when it was right in front of my face. I felt like I was in a dungeon. Then, the walls lit up. A warm glow filled the room.

"These are the walls of fire," And stated, "They are a way to replace torches. We don't use them in Millennia because they produce so much heat; but here they shouldn't be a problem for us. Also, I think you will both be happy to know that we have survived the Creature Chambers."

The walls only went up about ten yards. After that,

there was nothing. It looked like a dead end, and I could hear the sound of rushing water echoing off of the walls. I was nervous about what is was, but I kept my mouth shut. I didn't want to seem like a coward.

CHAPTER VII
ERIN

In my opinion, the Creature Chambers had been the hardest obstacle yet. I was relieved that we had finally passed it, but I was scared about what would be coming next. The fire walls were a blanket of heat, and until then I hadn't realized the maze was so cold.

Further ahead I heard the sound of rushing water. At first, I thought I was only imagining it; but it got louder as we walked down the tunnel. I wasn't the only one who could hear it.

Alex walked with his hands covering his ears, and And had his head bent down to reduce the noise. When we reached the end of the fire wall the floor started to become slippery, and mist floated through the air.

At the end, a huge waterfall stood right in front of us. The water was shallow; I could see rocks on the bottom and on the edges where they poked out of the water. My stomach churned. I had never liked the idea of freefalling, but now I needed to be okay with it.

And bent over and ran his hand along the wall, "It's too slippery for us to climb, so we're going to have to jump."

"And," Alex complained, "The water is too shallow. We are going to kill ourselves if we try to jump."

"We could, but the risk is much greater if we climb down the walls. If we fall, we'll fall onto the rocks and kill ourselves. Just remember, I am not the one who lost the long rope in the Creature Chambers. And the one we have left would never be long enough to get us down safely," he argued.

"Fine," Alex agreed, "but you have to go first."

"No problem," And stood for a few brief moments. Then he pushed off the side of the wall, and started falling towards the ground.

When he landed, there was a loud splash. He stood in shoulder high water. From above the water looked like it would be much shallower. There must have been some sort of optical illusion to scare people from jumping. However, before I could give much thought to it, And called out to me.

"Erin," he said, "jump; don't worry I'll catch you."

I fully trusted And, but that didn't take away any of my fear. The longer I looked down, the further I had to go. It took me a while before I finally closed my eyes and jumped.

Once I finally jumped I wasn't scared anymore. I felt like I was flying through the air, and I kept my eyes closed until I stopped falling. And caught me, just as he promised.

"You can open your eyes now," he whispered. When I opened them, they were instantly drawn to the waterfall. Looking up made the distance between here and the ledge appear much smaller. In fact, it was only ten or fifteen feet.

And set me on top of a rock so my head would stay above water. The water was cold, and the warmth from the fire walls instantly vanished from my body. And yelled at Alex until he finally jumped.

All of us were shivering, and we sat on a large, flat rock together. We weren't in the water anymore, but the spray from the waterfall drenched us.

We sat close together in a small circle for two reasons. The first was an attempt to keep warm, and the second was so we could actually hear each other. The sound of rushing water was overwhelming and ear-shattering.

"What are we going to do now?" my teeth chattered when I spoke.

"We have to go down the river and see what happens," And put his arms around me, "Hopefully we can find some sort of raft or boat to go on. The water is freezing, and I wouldn't be surprised if it was occupied by a serpent or two."

"Serpents?" I worried.

"Yes, but they'll leave us alone. Not very many of them can survive in water this shallow. I doubt there even are any right now, but if the water deepens we could start to cross paths with them."

Alex spoke up, "Now I think we should search around the rocks for something to float on."

"Yes," And said, "You can search the rocks to the left, and Erin and I will search to the right and near the waterfall. We can meet back here in ten minutes."

Alex set off to the left while And and I started searching the right. We found a lot of random pieces of wood. We assumed they were the remains of old boats and we tossed them up onto the rock.

Then we started towards the waterfall. And told me I didn't have to come if I was cold, but I protested and told him he couldn't go without me. He seemed happy that I wanted to come.

When he said, "Come along," he had a genuine smile on his face.

There was nothing on either side of the waterfall, so I suggested we search underneath it. And complimented me for thinking outside the box, and it's a good thing I had. On the wall behind the waterfall, there was a long, narrow hole in the wall. When we reached it, we realized there was a large canoe inside.

"Nice work," And high-fived me.

"Thanks," I smiled, "But I totally wouldn't have thought of it if it weren't for Annie."

"How did she help you find it?" he sounded confused.

"When we were little we used to play by a waterfall on the far end of the island," I began, "Annie wanted to know what was behind it because she read some story where fairies lived behind waterfalls. I was fascinated with her theory, so I decided to go along with her plan. When we got to the other side of the waterfall, there was nothing out of the ordinary. There was only a rock ledge. We still thought it was magical, and we went there every day together. After a while Annie became bored with it, and she wouldn't go there with me anymore. I visited less and less until I practically forgot about it. I haven't thought about those days for a while."

"It sounds like you and your sister are really close," he commented.

"Yeah; until I met you and Alex, Annie and my family were like the only people I really talked to or spent time with," I admitted.

"Before I met you," And smiled, "Alex and my family were the only people I actually enjoyed spending time with or talking to."

"I like spending time with you, too," I desperately wanted to ask him about Kate, but this wasn't the right time and I didn't want to ruin the moment.

"I guess we should get the canoe out of the wall," the tone of his voice told me he wanted to talk more but didn't know what to say, "Alex is probably wondering where we are."

We had to pull with our whole body weight just to make it rock back and forth. It was heavier than I was expecting it to be, and I was surprised when it didn't sink like a rock. Alex was already waiting for us when we got back to the rock.

He had collected a pile of wood. The pieces were

small, cracked, and full of splinters. When he saw the canoe his jaw dropped. He rushed over to help us push it, and with his help we made it to the rock in a matter of seconds.

"Wait," Alex surprised me. And and I both stopped moving, and he came up to me. I wasn't really in the mood for it. My arm was killing me, and I was dying to sit down. I thought I had hurt myself when we were pulling the canoe out, but I was wrong.

"What's wrong?" And demanded.

"We missed a stinger," Alex responded. I felt his hand on my back. It was cool from the water, and I could still feel it after he moved away. There was a sharp pain in the back of my right shoulder. I fought the urge to cry out in pain, and when it stopped, Alex stepped back. He held a stinger in his hand.

"That's impossible," And protested, "We got all of them in the Creature Chambers. There's no way we missed one, and if we did she would have felt it."

"I guess they don't affect everyone the same way," Alex offered.

"Oh, well," I interjected, "It's gone now. We should just keep moving. None of us know how long this river is and it is going to be night before we know it." I have no idea why, but I felt guilty for not telling them about the pain in my arm; and I didn't want them to know I had kept it from them.

"You're right," And said, "Alex, hand me the stinger. It might come in handy later." Alex did as he was told, and we climbed in the boat.

And and Alex paddled. They wanted my arm to rest

after having a stinger in it for such a long time. I wanted to help, but my arm was sore and I was tired. For once, I didn't argue. I couldn't reach where the stinger actually was, but the skin on my sides was rough and had small indentations. I imagined my back looking like a giant spider web.

As the river got deeper, I imagined a dozen sea monsters climbing into the canoe and trying to kill us. And said very few serpents can survive in shallow water, and this kept my mind at ease. Then, I started to see movement in the water.

"What was that?" I tried not to sound scared, but I sounded like a little girl in a horror movie.

"That was the lowest ranked serpent, an electric eel," And's voice quavered near the end. Something was wrong.

"Is it going to kill us?" I gulped.

"That particular one won't," he contemplated whether or not to tell me what he was thinking, "It will bring back others, and when they have strength in numbers they will attack."

It didn't take long for the eel to return. When And said it would bring back others, I thought he meant one or two more. Clearly I was wrong; at least thirty or forty eels had surrounded the canoe. Now they were waiting for their next direction.

"Get away from any metal if you don't want to be shocked to death," And demanded.

"If we can't fight them with our knives, then how are we supposed to defend ourselves?" Alex questioned.

"Use the paddle," And sounded like a ruthless dictator. I was surprised when he didn't add "you idiot" onto the end of his sentence.

I didn't have a paddle, so I pulled up one of the boards I had been sitting on. The nails crumbled in my hands when I pulled them out. Hopefully the boat would hold up better than the seats. I stood with And and Alex, waiting for the eels to rush towards us.

For the first few minutes, nothing happened. Then a sharp hiss pierced the air. They advanced towards us like miniature sea soldiers. The eel that made the hissing noise was by far the largest, but it stayed back while the others moved forward. This had to be the leader. I kept an eye on it, just to make sure I was right.

The eels knew we were avoiding metal, so they jerked the boat back and forth. We swung at them with our homemade weapons, but they dove under the boat and appeared on the other side.

I heard the faint hissing noise of the lead eel, the noises were battle instructions. We needed to kill it, before its army killed us. The battle was tied, but it wouldn't be for long.

"We need to kill the leader if we want to destroy the army," And called out.

"Easy," I told him, "it's the big eel over there," I gestured in the eel's direction.

"Are you sure?" he asked.

"Positive," I answered, "Every time it hisses, the others respond with an action."

"That's the leader in command then," he removed

the stinger from his pocket, "but he won't be for long. I am going to kill him."

On the count of three, he stopped fighting. Alex and I were left to fight alone. Alex took And's paddle and fought with both hands. He was more efficient than before, but the eels were in the position to win.

And had the stinger in his hand, and he was aiming it right at the leader. He kept adjusting his hand to be more accurate, and I wanted to scream at him to hurry up. We couldn't hold the eels off forever, and we certainly didn't have time for And to be taking this much time.

Finally he released the stinger. It shot straight through the air directly at the leader.

Just as it plunged into the eel's eye, another eel flung itself into the canoe. We scrambled away from it, and started paddling down the stream.

The other eels were in shock. We had just enough time to get past them. And said they wouldn't follow us without a leader to guide them, and the eel in the boat would dry up and die soon enough.

Now, all three of us were paddling. And and Alex had actual paddles, and I had my homemade weapon. We were moving faster than before, but the eel in the boat kept me on edge. It was twitching, and I wasn't sure if it was dying or preparing to attack. I hated the thought of death, but I hoped it would just die already. Then I could stop worrying about it.

When it finally stopped moving we stopped to release it into the water. The river had widened, and there was a small rock path on both sides. If walking wasn't slower, I would have gotten out of this boat a long time ago. Alex held onto the side of the path, meanwhile And leaned down to pick up the eel.

"If it starts to shock me," he told us, "you two have to hit me with the paddles. If you grab onto me with your hands, the electricity will flow into your body and kill you, too. One death is better than two or three."

Alex and I watched like hawks as he picked up the eel. He was about to drop it in the water when it began to shock him. Alex kept hold of the wall with one hand, and he swung at And with the other.

I wrapped both hands around the other paddle, and I hit And as hard as I could. His hand was stuck to the eel with concrete. I paused before striking at his hands. Alex did the same thing, and the impact made the eel go flying. It landed on the far rock path with a spark.

And was still shaking, and we pulled him over to the path. We sat on the edge, and kept our feet in the canoe (to keep it from drifting). It was nice to be out of the boat, but I was worried about And. He looked like a prisoner of war who had just been released.

"Are, are you alright?" I stuttered. There wasn't an immediate response, which worried me.

"I think so," he finally answered, "I'm just a little shocked," he smiled. He thought he was very clever. Normally I would have been slightly annoyed, but right now I couldn't have asked for anything better.

"That's good," I ran my hand up and down his back.

He leaned towards me and whispered, "I'm lucky to have you two. Not many people would care about me as much as you two do."

"You get what you give. You care about us, and we care about you. That's how family works," Alex stated, "And just so you know, Erin, I consider you just as much a part of my family as anyone else."

"I'm glad you think that because you're my family, too. If I don't see my parents or sister again, I'll have you guys, and that will be enough," I meant every word I said.

We climbed back into the boat and continued down the river. I felt like we had been paddling for hours. All of us were tired, and we were going to have to stop and rest soon. We hadn't stopped since before the Creature Chambers.

It had been more than a day since I'd eaten anything. Hunger gnawed at my stomach, and I couldn't wait to reach the end of the river. The further we went, the louder my stomach growled. If the water wasn't so loud, I'm sure And and Alex would have heard it.

The river started to narrow, and I got excited. I thought we were at the end. I paddled with more force, but when we turned the corner I was disappointed. We hadn't reached the end yet.

The river didn't only fan back out, but it turned into a large pond-like area. In the center, there was a whirlpool. It pulled in everything from all directions. We steered to the side where there was a wide ledge. We sat on the edge, and I watched objects spin and disappear in seconds.

"There's no point in trying to pass this today," And spoke, "We need to rest, and I think we should get some food into our systems." When he talked about eating, he looked right at me. If it had been any other situation, I might have felt embarrassed, but I was starving. I didn't care as long as I got to eat something.

We hauled the boat up onto the ledge, and sat down beside it. We ate slowly. Our food was going quickly, and we still hadn't found a way to replace it. We didn't set up camp; it was pointless if we were leaving as soon as we woke up. No one kept watch, so we all got a full night of sleep.

Every so often, a few drops of water would spray onto the ledge. I slept covered in a blanket to stay dry. Even though I was tired, it took me a while to fall asleep. I lay still and watched the water swirl around in the whirlpool.

Eventually I fell asleep. I don't know when, but the next morning And and Alex had to wake me up. I opened my eyes and slowly sat up. I wanted more time to sleep, but I was anxious to get past the whirlpool.

"I'm guessing you slept well," Alex smiled, "it took us like ten minutes to wake you up."

"Sorry," I groaned, "It took me a while to fall asleep."

"Well, you're up now. You should get something to eat. Today we have to sail around the serpent lair's entrance," And interjected. I knit my eyebrows in confusion; I had no idea what a serpent lair was. And and Alex had to explain it to me while I was eating.

"Strong serpents live in the water hundreds of feet deep," they started, "so they create whirlpools to catch prey. Small, weak serpents believe they will become strong and powerful if they survive the whirlpool. In reality, they become extra food. We have to careful if we don't want to become a serpent meal."

"Okay," I quavered, "This sounds like it will be interesting."

"It will," they agreed. We pulled the boat back into the water, and we started to pile all of our stuff into it. We were about to get into it when we got a few surprise visitors. I started freaking out because I thought they were serpents, but I was wrong.

They were dolphins. And and Alex seemed overjoyed, but I wasn't sure what was so great about this. After they finished explaining, I felt like a complete idiot. We would ride the dolphins to get around the whirlpool.

The maze creators had intended for this to happen. The people in ancient Millennia were extremely fond of dolphins, and it was very practical because the dolphins would eat some of the smaller serpents.

We slid off the ledge onto the dolphins' backs. In total there were five of them. We rode on the three largest. One of the smaller ones swam in front of us while the other one stayed behind us.

The dolphins were not like anything I had seen in pictures before. Those were a grayish color, and these were a dark, bold purple with flakes of shimmery silver. They were slippery to the touch, and I had to wrap my arms around its neck to avoid falling off.

The dolphins were strong, but slow. I was nervous. The current was pulling us closer and closer to the whirlpool, and the dolphins were starting to shake. I thought riding an exotic creature, like a dolphin, would be fun and exciting. Instead it was terrifying.

By now the ledge was just as far away as the other side. We couldn't turn back now, it was pointless. The dolphin dove down, and my head was covered in icy water. I tried to push myself upward, but I was frozen.

The dolphins were able to move much faster underwater, but the blood in my veins froze. My skin was numb, and I felt like I had spent a year trapped in a giant freezer. If this was the end I would die frozen, still, and unchanged.

I gasped for air, and relief washed over me when my lungs filled with oxygen. We were almost there. Every second we came closer. The water was shallow, so we were able to walk on our own. The dolphins left us, and they were blurs swimming back to the other side.

"That was so awesome," Alex was still psyched about the dolphins.

"Yeah," And agreed. Both of them were dry. I was completely drenched.

"How did you stay totally dry?" I demanded.

"We didn't slip and fall. You must have not been holding on tight enough," And laughed.

"I was perfectly fine when it came to holding on," I responded, "It isn't my fault that I had to ride on a dolphin who likes swimming underwater."

And and Alex started cracking up again. At first I wanted to yell at them that it wasn't funny; but I ended up laughing with them instead. I was shivering and my teeth chattered. I wasn't sure why, but that always happened when I got cold. There was no way for me to stop it.

And wrapped his arms around me and lifted me out of the water. I felt warmer knowing he was the one holding me; it felt like he was protecting me against all the bad things in the world. My teeth stopped chattering, and my skin was full of warmth.

When we reached the end of the water And set me down. He was stronger than I thought. To him, carrying me was as easy as lifting a cotton ball. He wrapped a blanket around my shoulders, but I already felt as warm as the sun.

CHAPTER VIII
ALEX

Things were becoming more complicated. Our first roadblock had just been a gate, but now we were navigating ice cold rivers and battling serpents. And and Erin kept forgetting I was there, and everything was beginning to annoy me. I was once the middle person, but now I was a third wheel.

We sat near the edge of the water and discussed what to do next. None of us knew if the water in the stream was safe to drink or not, and we didn't want make the wrong choice. If the water was clean we could easily refill our supply, but if it wasn't we could be dead within minutes. This was a rare opportunity, but the decision was risky.

"Why don't we just pour all of our clean water into a few bottles? Then, we can refill the rest with water from the stream?" Erin suggested.

"I guess that would work, we just need to find a way to differentiate between the bottles. If there is no way for us to tell them apart, we could end up in major trouble," And confirmed.

"We could put a small rock in the bottom of the ones with stream water," I proposed.

"I don't have any objections to that," Erin approved. She looked at And to back her up, and her thirst for his approval made something steam up inside of me. I didn't know if it was anger or if it was jealousy. The line between the two was very unclear.

It was hours before we started to head down the tunnel. Like always, And and Erin were together and I was on my own. We had been cautious about our water, so we only had to find two small rocks. The idea was much simpler than it turned out to be.

There were almost no loose rocks anywhere around the stream, and the ones that were loose were too big. And and Erin shared my bad luck. They hadn't even found a loose rock, let alone a small pebble.

In the end we used the side of a knife to pry small pebbles up from the bottom of the stream. Again, this was a whole lot easier said than done. We had to get them from the stream floor because it was the only place with small enough rocks.

The rocks were held to the stream floor by a thick layer of clear rock. We had to scrape at the floor and it peeled away one thin layer at a time. The pebbles we found were not what I was expecting.

One was a dark, eye-catching, fiery red. It was

round and smooth like a marble. The layers were hard and couldn't be broken. We dropped it into one of the bottles, and it sank slowly to the bottom.

The other was a clear blue color. It was roughly the shape of a star, and it was as thin as a sheet of paper. Although it was so thin, it was as strong as a diamond. This rock didn't sink. It floated at the top of the bottle and moved as if it was part of the water.

The containers were heavier than concrete. I could barely move without crumpling to the ground. I set my bag down every time I got the chance. My gut told me it wasn't safe to drink, but my brain told me to save it. It might become of great use to us.

It wasn't long before we came across another roadblock. We reached it after a couple short turns. For once I was happy to stop. I dropped my backpack on the ground and sat down next to it.

There was an arch that reminded me of the Creature Chambers, but there was no door. Ahead of us was an endless, narrow room. From where I was, it looked like it was filled with string. I sat up and started crawling towards it; I was anxious to see if I was correct.

I had almost reached it when And told me to stop. I froze in place. I didn't understand why he wanted me to stop. For a moment I considered ignoring him, but instead I turned around. I felt like a coward for following directions like a pet.

Coming back was embarrassing. I was like a child who had just been yelled at by a parent. I should have been brave enough to stand up to And. As usual, he and Erin were sitting side-by-side when I got back. They were discussing what the room was.

"Why did you tell me to stop?" I demanded. Those few simple words were a small victory for me. If I couldn't stand up to him I needed to at least call him out when he made a bad choice.

"That might look like a simple string maze, but we can't just cut our way through," And began, "It's actually filled with spider webs."

"How do you know that?" my simple victory shattered to the floor. I should have been the one to figure that out.

"Sit down," he waited for me to sit before he continued, "Do you see the first set of string — the shimmery white?"

"Yeah," I grumbled.

"That is the web of a white widow. You can tell by looking at the color and the pattern," And explained.

"So what," I huffed.

"If there is a white widow on the web, it could kill you before you even knew it was there." I hated it when And knew more than me.

"Well, if you're the expert, then how do you think we should get across the room?" I challenged him.

"First, we have to make sure there are no spiders. If we see one, we need to kill it. And if we're too far away to kill it, we can wait until it's asleep. Then, we have to pass through the webs as carefully as possible. If we touch one, it could alert another spider." He talked as if it were a simple plan.

"What about the purple webs?" I asked. I had never seen anything like it before, so I assumed And hadn't either.

"I have no idea what kind of spider made that web," he confessed, "but I think we should be just fine if we use the same plan."

"Whatever," I answered.

I looked across the room at the layers of webs. I wasn't sure how many layers there were, but I kept seeing reflections. I knew there was at least one more layer I couldn't see.

The floor was a metallic pink color. Pictures of spiders had been carved into it, and words were written around the edges of the room. They were dark black, and the color looked as bright and bold as a fresh coat of paint.

The ceiling was very similar, but it only had one symbol in the center. The edges were lined with pictures of spiders, and there were no words. It was steel gray, and the symbols looked like they had been painted with blood. It was smeared around the edges, and looked like it was fading.

I didn't recognize any of the languages the words were written in, so I assumed that they were ancient languages. Maybe they hadn't even been discovered by the people of Millennia. There were some languages that were unknown to anyone in the city, so we usually guessed what the words were trying to tell us. Their true meaning would be forever kept a secret.

"Let's go before anything bad happens," And suggested.

"That's exactly what I was thinking," Erin smiled

and slightly tilted her head. A piece of hair fell over her eyes, and she casually pushed it behind her ear.

We walked towards the spider webs until our faces were all but inches away from them. They smelled sour and the air around them tasted bitter. My eyes started watering, and I had to force them open.

I glanced back and forth across the room, but I couldn't see any spiders. I wondered if they had died off or if I had missed them. And and Erin were both squinting, but it looked like they hadn't seen anything either.

"I don't see any," I confirmed.

"Same," Erin agreed. And's face told me he hadn't seen any either. He was also worried, but for what reason I might never know.

"Why do you look so worried?" I questioned him.

"I don't see anything," he answered, "We're either very lucky, or we are walking into a death trap."

"Well, somebody is just bursting with optimism. Everything is going to be okay. If we can make it this far we can make it to the end," Erin sounded very convincing, but And was still worried.

"You are right," he said, "Let's just go through as quickly as possible. This place is kind of starting to creep me out." He turned away from us, leaving his face hidden in the shadows.

Erin grinned, "Who's first?"

And went first. He said it was because we needed to watch him, but I know he was lying. He kept his knife in his hand, and he never took his eyes off of the spider webs. He looked like a spy trying to get through a room full of laser beams.

He moved swiftly through the mess of webs. He never stopped moving, and soon he became a blur in the distance. He was constantly ducking and leaping around the webs. He never even came close to brushing one of them.

When he reached the small area between the white and purple webs he stopped moving. His eyes scanned the room for anything out of place.

When he was done, he called out for the next person to come. I hadn't really been paying attention when he crossed because I was too busy trying to read his expressions. I was nervous about figuring it out on my own, so Erin and I went together.

She was ahead of me by a few feet at any given moment. Watching her maneuver around the webs made it easier for me to pass them. Erin was as graceful as a ballerina. I could never copy her movements perfectly, but at least we were making progress quickly.

As we advanced, the webs became more and more tangled. The number of strings doubled, and the spaces between them were growing smaller and smaller. It came to a point where the spaces we had to duck through were so small that we had less than an inch of space for mistakes.

Erin was smaller than me, so she was able to squeeze through the small openings fairly easily and quickly. It took me more time, and she had to help me get through so I could avoid touching any of the webs.

We were almost there, and the openings allowed us no room for error. Erin was still able to slip past them, but when I tried I was not as lucky. My elbow brushed one of the webs, and it stuck. I tried to pull myself free, but the web was like glue sticking to my hand.

"Erin, wait!" I yelled, "Help me!" When she saw what had happened she snaked through the webs quicker that I had thought was possible. She was by my side within seconds. And was close behind her.

"What happened?" she demanded as soon as she reached me.

"My elbow barely brushed one of the webs, and now it's stuck," the words flew out of my mouth as they formed in my head. My voice was full of panic. I tried to calm down and say it again, but it was still almost impossible to comprehend.

Luckily, Erin seemed to understand what I said this time. And finally reached us and Erin was explaining what happened. And's eyes darted across the room. He was expecting a spider to appear out of nowhere and attack us any minute.

"I'm starting to think there aren't spiders here," And sounded relieved, "I think the obstacle is that the webs stick to your skin. Finding out how to free you is going to be a challenge."

I had to do this by myself. If And and Erin got stuck trying to help me, we would be out of luck. We would be stuck there forever. I tried everything, but the web wouldn't loosen its grip on me at all. I thrust my arm back as hard as I could, and tried to twist out of the web. None of my efforts made a difference.

"It's not going to be an obvious thing," And stated, "The maze was built to be impossible for anyone to figure out without a map."

"We could try to cut the web," Erin offered.

"If we did that we would probably lose a knife," And said, "We'll need them to fight against the cannibals eventually, so we have to find another way." He was calm. I could have died, but my brother wouldn't waste a knife to save me. To him this was no big deal.

There was a long silence while we were thinking of ways to cut the web, but none of them seemed practical. It wasn't until I became thirsty that it hit me.

"We can use the thin, blue rock from the stream. We put it in a bottle of water. It's definitely sharp enough to cut through the web!" I exclaimed.

And agreed, "Turn around so I can get it out of your backpack."

Erin unzipped my backpack, and And pulled out the bottle of water. He slid the blue stone between his fingers, and put the water back into my backpack. He wrapped it up in a blanket so we would know that it was stream water.

I pulled my arm back to make the string taught. The stone fit perfectly between And's fingers, and when he touched the blue stone to the web it instantly snapped. All of the webs stopped shimmering and fell to the floor like chains of snowflakes.

We all braced ourselves to be covered in the sticky webs, but they didn't cling to us like magnets. When we broke the web and it stopped shimmering, the stickiness went away, too. We pulled the webs off of ourselves and piled them in a corner.

Then, we walked towards the purple webs. And

slid the blue stone in the pouch with his knife. This time we knew there were no spiders, so we walked across the room without a single worry.

All three of us went together this time. The webs were arranged like the last ones, but these weren't sticky. We ducked and crawled under each web until we were in the center of all the purple webs.

We couldn't move anymore. The webs had wrapped themselves around our feet, and they were working their way up. If we didn't escape them soon, they would suffocate us. Forcefully we pulled our feet in all directions, but the webs wouldn't snap. We tried to cut through them with our knives and the blue stone, but they wouldn't break.

"Keep moving, you can't stop," And hollered. I wanted to tell And he was being an idiot. I couldn't move, but And was almost free of the webs. I created as much movement as possible, and it wasn't long before I realized movement caused the webs to loosen.

Finally, the webs were loose enough for me to step out of their grasp. And was free, and now he was helping Erin. She was the shortest, so she had gotten the most tangled. Webs were wrapped all around her feet, and they continued up to her waist.

I stood on top of the webs above the floor so I couldn't be tangled again. Then, I walked along it like a tightrope until I reached And and Erin. Now, the webs were only to her knees, but more and more kept grabbing a hold of her. If And hadn't had his arm around her, she probably would have fallen. After that, she would have become covered within seconds.

At last And lifted her out of the webs. He climbed up onto the rope next to mine, and he set Erin on the next web over. The webs on the ground were still moving back and forth like snakes waiting for one of us to fall so they could kill us. At first we sat down and slid across the webs because it seemed the safest.

However, it wasn't long before And stood up and grabbed onto the next layer of webs to steady himself. I did the same thing, but Erin was too short to reach the next layer. And offered her a piggy-back ride and she gratefully accepted it.

While we were walking, the two of them were chatting and laughing the whole time. I tried to listen to what they were saying, but I couldn't focus. My mind kept drifting back to reality. I had become the third wheel.

I was grateful when the webs began to thicken. The webs above us were short enough for Erin to hold onto now, so I didn't feel as left out. The downside was, And and I were too tall to stand now. I had to bend my knees and lean back. I felt like an awkward limbo dancer.

This was very uncomfortable, and I had to pause so I could catch my balance. Again, I was jealous of Erin. She was able to walk with the slightest bend in her knees and keep her back straight. She held on above her with both hands, and she never had to stop and regain her balance.

And was in the middle of us. He couldn't do the limbo-thing like I was. He was too tall, and the front of his shirt kept getting caught on the webs. Crawling was too dangerous, because you couldn't balance, so he had to lay flat on his stomach. His hands were on the same web as his body, and he reached forward and pulled himself forward over and over again.

I was the last one to reach the end of the purple webs, and in front of us was a third set of webs. This last set was a reflective gold. It wasn't shiny like the white had been, but light bounced back and forth between the strands.

I felt a sense of pride for being correct. And and Erin seemed surprised that there was a third set of webs. I was the only one who had anticipated them. However, I was also disappointed. This meant that we hadn't finished the obstacle yet. My pride was washed away with frustration. All I wanted was to get out of here.

"Before we start charging through like we did last time," Erin said, "We should figure out what exactly these webs do." A shiver went down her spine; the webs had left a lasting impression on her. She tried to hide her discomfort, but And sniffed it out like a bloodhound.

"I think you're right, we'll be more cautious this time. I promise," And pulled Erin towards him and held her tightly with one hand. He reached for the blue stone with his other hand and stroked it along the nearest web. When nothing happened he tossed it into the middle of the room. We waited for a few moments, but still nothing happened.

"The webs are as hard as steel bars," And confirmed, "but other than that, I don't see why they would be a threat to us."

We decided to climb through the webs like we did last time. There weren't as many webs here, and they were very spaced out. There were only a few narrow spaces we had to go through.

This section was huge. It was over twice the size of the other two combined, and at the end of it I only saw a wall. The room must have been connected to multiple hallways at the end. When we finally reached the end of the web, I thought it was over. We had gotten through with no difficulty, but there was still more to go.

In front of us was not a wall as I had thought. It was a net-like spider web that blocked the way out. Behind it I could see a narrow tunnel. In the middle of it was a walkway, and there were cliffs on both sides of it. The drop was so far I couldn't see where it ended.

I really hoped that we wouldn't have to jump again. I never would have admitted it, but I was deathly afraid of heights. If it hadn't been for And and Erin I would have ended up wandering around and looking for another way through the maze. In there, searching could be suicide. It was best to just go in a straight line. It made it harder to get lost that way.

"Do you guys know how we're going to get past this huge net thingy?" And questioned. I looked around for a possible solution, but I couldn't see any. The ground was solid rock. It couldn't be broken or chipped away enough for one of us to pass through.

The webs were still as strong as steel cables, so there was no chance of breaking them. They ran all the way up to the ceiling, and there weren't any gaps we could fit through. We couldn't go over, under, around, or through. I didn't know how else we could get past it, but there had to be a simple solution. We just couldn't see it yet.

"Maybe there's a lever or something like there was at the gate," Erin suggested.

"It's possible," And replied, "but it could be anywhere in here, and there are millions of webs. Also the maze doesn't like to repeat itself, so I doubt that there would be two of the same solutions in less than the first ten obstacles."

"Could we bend them?" I asked.

"We could, but not with any of the supplies that we have," And shot down the idea. It didn't seem like we were getting anywhere so I took off my backpack and sat next to it.

I pulled out a container of water to get a drink, and when I pulled out the first container it was much heavier than it should have been. I immediately knew that it was the stream water. I had no idea why, but it was as heavy as concrete and it seemed to get heavier with every step I took.

"We should get rid of the water from the stream," I said.

"Why would we do that?" Erin asked, "It's not like we come across a stream every fifteen minutes."

"I know," I said, "but this water is way heavier than other water. It was also so convenient. Everything about it just seems shady. There's no way I'm going to drink it. It'll probably kill you instantly."

"What do you mean it's heavier than normal water?" Erin asked, "Water is water and it all has the same weight."

"No one told that to this water," I tossed her the

container. She easily caught it, but the weight pulled her down until she was sitting on the ground.

"Okay, I am so not drinking this," she informed, "I do not need to gain five pounds from drinking weird water. How did you even carry those containers; they must be like a hundred pounds all together!?"

I laughed, "I guess you're just not as strong as me." She glared at me and stuck her tongue out instead of responding; it made me laugh even harder.

"Erin," And asked, "Can you pass me the container?" Erin tried to lift the container off of the ground, but it was too heavy for her to pick up. After a second she gave up and rolled it across the floor to him.

He lifted it up right before it hit his feet, and he weighed it in each hand. He twisted the cap off and examined the inside. He seemed confused about what could make it so heavy. He smelled it, and it looked like he was thinking.

At first I wondered if it smelled differently, but I didn't remember anything unusual about the way it smelled in the stream. Then, it had just smelled like any other water, but it had also not seemed as heavy as it was now, either. Something clicked in my mind, and I realized that it wasn't water. It was some other kind of liquid. One that changed based on what condition it was in.

And lifted the container above his head and hurled it towards the wall of webs. It struck the net with full force, and it shook slightly. The bottle stuck between two of the webs, and then it shattered. The liquid inside kept the shape of the bottle, but it began to flow out of shape and onto the webs.

It moved slowly, and it was as thick as syrup. In my mind I imagined it would be sticky. I wondered why And had thrown it at the web. If it was sticky then it would be even harder to get through. There was no reason behind his actions sometimes.

Eventually, the stream of liquid began to slow until the last drops spilled out of it. It had coated the webs beneath it with a hard shell. At first, I thought it was making the webs turn clear, but then I realized that they were shrinking.

There was a sizzling sound as the liquid from the bottle ate away at the webs. When the webs were gone, the hardened liquid began to crack. I watched the small cracks spread along the surface as they became larger and deeper.

The hardened liquid looked like shattered glass, but it seemed stronger. Then, the wall crumbled into a million pieces. It started at the bottom, and when it was finished it had formed a large pile on the ground. It looked like broken glass, but the sound of it shattering still bounced off of the walls. It was a powerful and unforgettable sound.

"What was that?" Erin shook in surprise.

"That was acid," And confirmed, "I would tell you what kind, but I am not quite sure how to pronounce it. Anyway, when it is cold enough, it is just like water. That's how it was in the stream, but when it heats up it thickens. It's so strong, it can burn through metal. But don't worry it can't harm humans in any way."

"I've never seen anything like it, how did you know about it?" Erin mused.

"It was invented in Millennia," And responded.

"Wow that was such a great explanation," Erin said, "I only have one question: can we just walk across it or do we have to jump over it or something?"

"We can just walk over it. Oh, and yes, I know I have quite a gift when it comes to explaining things," And answered, "Alex, you are going to have to jump because you lost one of your shoes and you don't want to cut your feet."

"That is not my fault," I complained.

"Actually it kind of is," Erin pointed out. This time I was the one to stick my tongue out and glare. We all started laughing, and we passed over the pile of hardened acid pieces. We headed down the hallway, and I'm not sure why, but I was eager for our next roadblock.

.

CHAPTER IX
ERIN

Although the webs had been a fairly easy obstacle I was ready to be out of there. Something about the entire thing sent tingles all the way through my body. I knew there weren't any spiders, but I was still always worried I would see one.

When we passed over the shards of hardened acid I heard loud cracking noises, and it felt like I was walking on ice. Anyway, what now stood in front of us was a long, narrow strip of walkway. On both sides there were long drops, and at the bottom of them I could make out the faint outline of pointed rocks. It looked like something from an evil lair in a little kid's movie.

It surprised me when And came to an abrupt stop. He had been walking in front of me and Alex was behind me. He turned around to us and put a finger over his lips. He was signaling for us to be absolutely silent. When there was no more noise, I heard what And had heard. There were voices in the distance.

"Come along, we must get to the diamond mine," the first voice was serious. "We don't want to keep our majesty waiting."

"Fine," the second voice grumbled, "Why do we have to get her diamonds anyway? It's not like anyone down here cares about their appearance."

The first voice spoke, "I think you are mature enough to know the truth, so I will tell you. But you mustn't tell anyone what I am about to tell you. The only people who know this are the majesty and her closest companions. In total there are five of us, and after I tell you there will be six. I expect it to stay at six afterwards, so if you open your big mouth you will be gone."

"I'm ready," the second voice commanded.

"Alright," the first voice began, "The diamonds are not for decoration, or anything that most people would think that they are for."

"What are they for then?" the second voice pleaded.

"Knowledge comes with patience," the first voice stated before continuing, "The diamonds are the key to the portals." There was a brief pause, "When you have a diamond from this diamond mine you can travel through portals. There is one located in every hallway of the maze, and they lead to all different places in the world. Some of them even go to the dark world. The diamonds last forever, unless you venture to the dark world. This is something our majesty does quite often. When they are used for that purpose, they can only be used twice. Once to get there, and once to leave. Another important thing about the diamonds is that they must be completely covered when you go through a portal. If they are not, the entryway will shatter and disappear. Anyone on the other side will be left there forever. Also, anything going through the portal will be sliced in half. The portals are very dangerous and powerful. That is why they must be kept a secret. Only diamonds from our mine can activate them; if you don't have one you will be lost in time forever."

"Why does our majesty venture to the dark world?" the second voice questioned.

"She is one of the Great Twenty-Four. I'm sure you were taught about them at one point. Everything you were taught is accurate, except for one thing. They are not myths. Our majesty is the leader, and she was the only one powerful enough to escape the dark world. The others were left behind, and they will remain there until their chosen one is found. The majesty visits the other twenty-three often. When she is not with them, she is searching for the chosen ones. When she finds them, she will take them to the dark world. Then, her siblings will rise once again by taking over and inhabiting the chosen ones' bodies. You must never let on that you know, but the majesty is weak. She has not found her chosen one yet, and if she doesn't find him soon she will have to return to the dark world. That is why she burned the maps of the maze and has turned it into her kingdom."

After that there was no more talking. Their footsteps came closer and closer to us. And pushed us back into the room of webs. We all had our knives in hand, but

And wouldn't let Alex and I come with him.

"Do not come out of hiding no matter what," he demanded. He rose to his feet and silently walked out of the room.

Still they had not reached us. And was stretching; we all knew there was going to be a fight. Alex and I climbed to the top layer of the webs and moved until we had found a position where we could observe what was going on below without being seen.

Nervous chills ran through my spine and filled my bloodstream. I knew this was a bad idea. Alex and I should be down there fighting with And. I wanted to move, but my brain felt disconnected from my body. I was frozen in place by fear.

I kept my eyes on And, and I never took them off of him. A voice in my head told me this could be the end of his journey, but I refused to acknowledge it. His muscles flexed with every move he made. His jaw was hard and set. His eyes were burning with rage.

The anticipation was killing me. I was almost relieved when I saw two creatures emerge from the shadows. The first thing I noticed was their eyes. They were endless black holes. Those were the eyes of a killer. There would be no mercy, only pain. Their skin was a green brown color. It was the smooth skin of a frog, and it was paper thin. You could see clouded images within it.

Long, thin fangs hung from the corners of their mouths, and their noses were long and narrow. They curled their mouths back and bared their teeth. The clouded images in their skin began to surface, and I could clearly make out the pictures. I knew exactly what was going to happen next.

They slowly began to change shape and become larger. When they stopped changing, they were something else entirely. They had become the creature that brought me to Millennia. I squeezed my eyes shut and opened them over and over again. I wanted all of this to be nothing more than a dream.

Memories from that night flooded my head, and I clung to Alex like a wet T-shirt. He put his arm around me and pulled me closer to him. My head was level with his shoulder, and I could feel his heart beating through his skin.

The simple repeated pulse calmed me. It filled my entire body with a false sense of warmth, but it was not relaxing enough. I wanted to turn around and pretend everything was alright. Shielding myself seemed like the best idea in the world. It's what I wanted, but I needed to watch. If I didn't I know I would have regretted it.

I tried to scream for And to run, but I couldn't make a sound. Alex covered my mouth tightly with his hand. I fought against him, but he was stronger than me. Throughout the rest of the day, I continually wondered what would have happened if I had gotten one word out of my mouth. I wondered if things would have played out differently. I liked to think what happened was unavoidable. That's because if I had come to a different conclusion, I would have been eaten away by guilt.

"Fresh blood," the smaller one cooed, "What are we waiting for?"

"Patience," the other voice was older and wiser,

"We must bring him to our queen. He could be among the chosen."

"It's not fair if you get your way all the time. You're probably just saving him for yourself, and I'm not going to let that happen," the first creature charged. And looked scared, and it made me tense. I had stopped trying to escape Alex's grip, so he had released me. I wiggled forward. I didn't want to watch this, but nothing could pull me away.

All eyes were locked on And, but he was confident. An audience didn't make him nervous, it made him better. Short claws shot out from below the creature's fingers, and reached towards And's face. They tore easily through the skin and left five shallow cuts behind. The cuts ran from the corner of his eye to his jaw. Blood flowed down his face and neck.

And lifted his knife and swung it towards the creature. It made a clean cut along its neck, and the creature screeched and howled in pain. Thick black blood bubbled out of the wound. It made a sizzling noise, and a small cloud of smoke formed. The other creature came rushing towards the fight.

The smaller creature tackled And, and they were rolling around on the ground. They were shredding each other to pieces. The sound of fighting filled the area. I heard the creature's claws scratch at And's knife. They were both crying out in pain and rage.

The larger creature yanked the smaller creature off of the floor. He was holding him by the skin on the back of its neck. The larger one began rapidly spitting out words, and the other creature's face filled with shock. They had both forgotten about And.

He took this opportunity to strike. He kicked out at the larger creature's ankles, and it came crashing down. They snarled at him, and then lashed out again. They were all moving so fast, I could never tell who was in the lead.

Red and black blood was spraying everywhere. I didn't want to fight, but I wanted to help And. I gave Alex a hopeful look that said, "Can we go help now?" He just shook his head and looked down.

The fight was sickening, but was impossible to tear my eyes away from. Everyone was screaming and shouting at each other. They used languages that were foreign to me. I was grateful that I didn't know what they were saying.

Then I saw one of the figures collapse to the ground. My heart stopped. I turned my head, and forced the tears to stay in my eyes. I didn't want to be weak. Alex was as still as a stone for a moment, but then he turned to me and mouthed, "Okay."

My heart started to pound. It wasn't because I was afraid or because I was tired. This was because I was relieved. I couldn't imagine my life without And, and I didn't know what I would do if I lost him.

I turned back to the fight. The larger creature had been killed, but the smaller one was still fighting for its life. And was slowing, and his opponent was gaining on him. They were getting closer to the edge, and every step they took towards it made my heart skip a beat.

And now stood with his heels on the edge. One more step, and he was gone. I couldn't decide if this was something I wanted to watch, or something I should turn away from. I closed my eyes, but I couldn't stand not knowing what was happening. I opened my eyes a little bit. I could only see what was right in front of me, but that was all I needed.

The creature wasn't smart. Its stupidity is what cost it its life. In one swift movement, it lunged at And. He didn't move out of the way fast enough, and they both disappeared off of the side of the walkway. It took me a moment to process. When it clicked, I wished it hadn't.

I called out, "NOOOOO!" Tears spilled out of my eyes and soaked my face. Alex gently stroked my back, and then we started to climb down. I needed to know what had happened. I hoped And had fallen on some sort of ledge. Something had to have saved him; he couldn't be gone.

I didn't bother climbing down; I leaped off of the edge and fell to the ground. When I hit it, pain shot up my legs. My whole body shook. I limped across the walkway with Alex beside me. I grabbed onto his hand and prepared myself to look down.

When I looked down, my tears stopped. And had his knife in the side of the walkway. It was the only thing keeping him from falling, but it was enough. I reached down and placed my hand over his. It felt warm and it was slick with sweat, but I didn't mind.

"We'll get you up," I reassured him.

"You can't," he struggled to speak. I was about to ask why not, but then I looked further down. The creature clung to And's leg, and it was slowly inching its way up.

"We'll find a way," my voice was meant to sound confident, but I was frustrated. I couldn't keep my fear buried any longer.

"No," And's response was the hard truth, "If I live, so will this." He shook his leg for dramatic effect, "I have to let go before it has a chance."

I squeezed And's hand. I didn't know what to say. I knew that he was right. He had to die; it was our only chance. It was him or all of us. I wanted to tell him we would all die fighting together, but I knew he was too selfless to accept that. In the end, I settled on three simple words to say.

"I love you," this time I sounded confident. There was no doubt in my mind. I loved him, and I always would. I had to tell him before it was too late.

"I will always love you," he spoke softly. There was nothing but truth in his voice. He leaned forward and kissed my hand. I knew I had to let go, but everything in my mind told me not to. I fed off of his strength as his fingers slipped out of mine. He plummeted into the darkness.

I would always remember this moment. It left me with the most painful scar in the world: a broken heart. But it also left me with an image in my mind — the image of a double arrow. And had the same mark on his wrist that I had on mine.

Questions were flying through my mind so rapidly that I was surprised I didn't end up with a concussion, "Could these identical marks have something to do with why I trusted And without question from the second we met? Could they be the reason why I fell for him so quickly and irrationally?" I had no idea what they meant, but I couldn't stop thinking of all the possibilities; and I knew I was going to find out — even if it was the last thing I did.

We never heard another word from And. Knowing he was gone was one thing, but accepting his death was something much more challenging. I couldn't believe that I was never going to see him again. His voice still lingered in my head. I will always love you. I had imagined him saying those words to me for days now. Now that he had said them, he was gone. He died exactly how he wanted to, protecting the people he loved. Protecting me.

Memories from my last few days with him rushed into my mind. I regretted being so unsure of myself. Wishing I'd told him how I felt sooner was the worst feeling in the world. I finally met someone I wanted to be with forever, and I blew it. I felt like a complete idiot. If I had been an ounce weaker, there would be nothing keeping me from jumping. If I couldn't be with him, I could die with him.

The only thing giving me strength was him. If I jumped, he would think I was a coward. I would no longer be the girl he loved. The girl he loved would make his death mean something. She would make sure someone paid for it. I wasn't going to back down. I was going to be the girl he fell for, even if it killed me inside. And I was going to find out what the double arrow meant. It couldn't be a coincidence. Nothing in the maze was ever a coincidence.

My sadness was then replaced with anger. I dried my face with my sleeve and leaned over the edge. The voice in my head told me I had to pull out his knife. It was painful, but that knife was one of the only pieces I still had of him. I gripped it tightly and slid his pack over my shoulder. I didn't mind the extra weight. It gave me something other than And for my mind to focus on.

I strode over to where And had his last moments. I used his knife and carved a small heart into the ground. Then, I ran the blade across my palm. A shallow cut was left behind, and I clenched my hand into a fist. Blood flowed out of the cut and fell to the ground. It stained the heart I'd drawn red. Now, part of me would always be with And.

When I finished, I started across the walkway. I was eager to get out of this place, and my head was spinning. For the first time, I hoped an obstacle would come soon. Maybe I would be able to get my mind off of And then. However, I had something to do first.

"What are you doing?" Alex hurried to catch up with me.

"Walking," I stated the obvious.

"I get that part," he sounded annoyed, "I meant where?"

"To the diamond mine," to me the answer was simple.

"Are you crazy!" he exclaimed, "You are going to get us both killed!"

"No," I said, "I'm going to get revenge. Those creatures need to know that they messed with the wrong girl. They will pay for And's death, and I'm going to be there when it happens. Oh, and I also want to know about these so-called portals."

Alex grinned in approval, and it was settled. We were going to go to the diamond mine. From there, we would figure out how to use the portals. Next, we planned to find Annie and Ria. With their help, we could take down whatever dark creatures had killed And.

I considered telling Alex about the double arrows, but something told me not to. I needed to find out what they meant by myself and I didn't want him to have a reminder of his brother every time he looked at me. He had enough to deal with as things were and I didn't want to put something else into his mind that he could think and obsess over.

CHAPTER X
ALEX

First Ria, and then And. I wished I knew what to do. It was clear to me when And was going to die. I just stood there and did nothing. The guilt was eating away at me. I was too optimistic. I set out thinking this would be the type of adventure people had in movies. Losing never seemed like something that could happen.

I had never even gotten to say goodbye to And. The opportunity was there, but I pushed it away. I didn't want to have to say goodbye, so I didn't. Now, all I wanted was to go back to that moment and say goodbye.

He was the only sibling I had left, and now he was gone. Nobody would ever be able to take his place. Erin might have been able to, but in my mind she'd already taken the place of Ria. As much as I cared about her, it was hard to be around her right now. I envied her more than anyone else.

She told And she loved him, and she hadn't even known him for a month. I had known him for my whole life! It wasn't fair. Why couldn't I say goodbye to him? Was it because she was more sensitive than me, or was she stronger?

Either way, I knew that this had to wait. I needed to focus on what was happening and what was about to happen. For now, I would have to leave the past behind. Erin could push her feelings away, but I couldn't. She could turn pain into fiery rage, and I was stuck waiting to be saved.

Tears were stockpiling in my eyes. I forced them back, but twice as many returned. Finally, I couldn't take it anymore. All of the tears fell at once and I didn't think they were ever going to stop. They ran down my face and stuck to my neck like sweat.

Erin immediately tried to comfort me. I was happy that she didn't say anything, and I didn't say a word in return. At first she hesitated. She wasn't sure what to do, but she ended up being exactly what I needed.

She sat down on the ground and motioned for me to sit next to her. When I sat, I cradled my knees to my chest and rocked back and forth. I was shaking, and my eyes were still leaky faucets. I was shivering, and I blew warm air into my hands.

Erin placed her hand on my back, and she ran it back and forth between my shoulder blades. Her hands were ice cold, but at the same time they felt warm and comforting. My neck and forehead were covered in a thin layer of sweat, and my palms felt cold and sticky.

She waited to speak until my breathing had evened out, "Everything is going to be okay. For all we know, he might not even be gone. I know it's a lot to take in, but you have to find a way to accept it. Otherwise, you'll never be able to move on. Remember, this isn't what he would have wanted. He would tell us to keep fighting and accomplish what we had set out to do. I know I didn't know him as long as you have, but it didn't take long to find out who he was. He was a good person, and we should do what he would want."

"Thank you," I stuttered, "I may have lost two siblings to this maze, but I also got one. It's worth it, and I wouldn't change anything." I meant every word I said, but it hurt to tell the truth. It made me feel like I was betraying my blood siblings.

And had been a great loss, but I could get past it. Erin on the other hand, would have been much harder to lose. I hated myself for caring more about a stranger than my own brother, but I couldn't change reality without lying to myself.

"Thank you," she added, "I don't want it to sound like his…death didn't affect me, but we can't change anything that happened. I think it's time for us to move on; we still have a lot of things we need to do."

I slowly rose to my feet, and I stumbled across the rest of the walkway. Fortunately, after the walkway we were back to walking through tunnels. The only difference was, this time we were looking for the diamond mine.

Even though this time we knew exactly where we wanted to go, I felt even more lost than before. We took turn after turn, hoping that we were going the right way. More than once, we had to turn around because we reached a dead end.

Now, we were on a path that only went one way. There were no options of which way we could turn, and I was glad we didn't have to make any decisions. We wound through the tunnel for miles and miles, and then it stopped.

This time we had not reached a dead end. We were standing in front of an entrance to an old abandoned mine. Pieces of dirt and rock were falling from the ceiling, and there was a pile of them on the ground. I had a feeling it wasn't safe. It felt like the ceiling was going to cave in at any moment.

"You ready?" I gulped.

"Yes," she didn't sound scared at all.

"Aren't you at least a little scared?" I felt like a coward.

"After everything else we've been through, it doesn't seem like such a big deal. Remember to look at the big picture. They would never make it seem like it was safe to go in here. If they did then every person who entered the maze would come here. The creators were smart. We need to have a little faith."

I was still uneasy, but I couldn't let her go in there alone. I cracked my fingers as we entered the mine. It was an old habit I had never been able to break. Even when I was a little kid, I cracked my fingers when I wasn't sure about something. It comforted me. At that moment, I thought I was going to get buried alive.

Once we entered, we were standing in a small room.

It had dirt floors, and the ceiling almost touched my head. After that, there was a short, narrow passage. We thought it would lead us into the actual mine. There was a beat-up wooden arrow pointing towards the passage, so we decided to give it a shot.

The passage was so small, Erin had to crawl. I had to slide on my stomach. It was pitch black, so we had no idea where we were going. I held onto one of Erin's ankles. We weren't going to risk being separated.

There were cobwebs everywhere. Dirt and dust showered down from the ceiling, and it covered us with a dozen fine layers. The route was not completely straight, so I had to keep one hand against the wall to guide me.

It felt like we were climbing over huge rocks. It was steep going up, and then it would drop down and become flat. All of the movement made me dizzy. The whole passage smelled like rotting food and smoke. I felt the urge to cough every time I took a breath, but I had to resist the urge. We needed to be as silent as possible. We didn't know if we were the only ones down here.

The path seemed to be endless. I was about to ask Erin if she was ready to turn around, but then I saw a small light. I immediately let go of Erin's ankle, and we rushed towards the light. I didn't care what else was there; I wanted to get out of this tunnel.

I felt invincible. It was like nothing in the world could touch me. Adrenalin rushed through my veins. I was ready for anything. When the tunnel finally ended, the opening was rough and narrow. We had to suck in our stomachs to fit through it.

I wondered how the cannibals that killed And could get through here. Both of them were much larger than any of us. If we could barely fit, they wouldn't have any chance of getting through. Although their majesty was weak, she must have still been able to give them power. This gave them the ability to change shape. We were up against something completely foreign.

I wanted to know if Erin thought my theory was right, but it would probably sound stupid if I said it out loud. This was probably a fake entrance. The arrow would never point to the main one. We must have missed it. When we were out of the passageway, we were in a long, octagonal-shaped room. The ceilings were still low, so we had to duck as we moved.

We melted into the shadows, and I searched the room to make sure we were alone. I felt vulnerable. It was still dark, and I couldn't see anything that wasn't right in front of me. My mind kept playing tricks on me and showing me images that weren't real.

There were large piles of diamonds, and there was a single figure bent down over a pile. As my eyes focused on it, I realized that it was a cannibal. I stopped moving and stared at it. I was closely watching its every movement. I didn't know if this was real or just my imagination.

It stood up, and a piece of light caught its face. The light came from its hand. In it, there was a large stone-like shape. I knew it had to be a diamond. It moved its hand up and down, as if weighing it, and then it walked across the room towards one of the walls and disappeared.

Erin and I knew this was our chance. There

wouldn't be another chance to be alone in the mine. We went to the pile where the figure had been. I picked up everything that could be a diamond. We filled every empty space in our backpacks, and when we turned towards the wall it was covered in mirrors. Light flowed through them, and I was drawn towards them.

There was no way a mirror could be a portal, it wouldn't make sense. Yet, this was right in front of us, proving us wrong. We lifted one of them off of the wall. We thought this was how to enter the portal. We waited and waited, but nothing happened.

When the mirror became too heavy to hold, we hung it back on the wall. I grabbed another jewel from the pile next to us. Maybe I had just gotten a bad diamond. A new one could show me the portal.

The mirror lit up around the edges with gold and silver sparkles, and the center was as bright as the sun. Heat floated off of the surface, and it filled me with a sense of warmth. At first, I was so startled that I dropped the diamond.

My eyes watched it fall. When it hit the ground, everyone would know we were here. I wanted to stop it, but it was falling too fast. There was no way I could stop it. When it hit the ground a loud earth-shattering noise drifted upward. It was a wonderfully dreadful sound I can still hear inside of my mind.

I heard footsteps coming from the entryway. I scooped the diamond off of the floor, and pulled Erin through the portal with me. When we passed through, the light was blinding. I felt like I was floating inside of a fire.

It was a terrible feeling, but as soon as it was gone I wanted it back.

We ended up in a dark room. It was so dark that I couldn't see my own hand in front of my face. I shifted to the side, and I pressed my back against the wall. I could hear Erin breathing softly next to me.

I would have tried to destroy the portal, but I didn't want to draw any more attention towards us, especially when I didn't know if it would work or not. Just as I began to relax, the sound of whispers floated towards us. My hand flew to my knife.

Although I couldn't see anything, I was sure my knuckles were turning white. I felt like I couldn't loosen my grip even if I wanted to. I had begun to worry we'd reached more cannibals. After what happened last time, I knew they would want to fight to the death.

"What are those?" the first voice sounded angry and fierce.

"They're gems," the answer was weak and scared.

"Why are not all of them diamonds?" the tone of voice sent chills through me. Erin grabbed onto the sleeve of my shirt. We didn't dare make a sound.

"It-it was d-d-dark an-an and I couldn't see," the second voice trembled.

"Do you know what the other gems do?" the first voice taunted. I felt like it was going to give away some priceless information. Then, it would kill the other voice for its own enjoyment. Being filled with incredible knowledge would make its death even more painful and meaningful.

"N-n-no," the other was breathing hard in fear.

"Well," the response was smooth as silk, "emeralds allow one to see portals, but not actually pass through them. Therefore, they are considered the least desirable," the voice threw a gem towards the wall, "Next, there are sapphires. They give the ability to pass through a portal. However, you cannot see it. They can be quite useful for making a dramatic exit, but that is not what I want," another gem flew towards the wall, "Ah, then the rubies. These are the second most powerful. They allow the one possessing them to travel through a portal, and they can see it at the same time. Lastly, we have diamonds. They are the most powerful and desirable. This is because you can see portals, pass through them, shatter them to conceal your path, and they make you aware of the dark portals." There was a slight pause as it stopped to catch its breath, "There are only a few dark portals in existence, and without a diamond there are none. These are the portals that lead to the dark world. It is dangerous to go there, but you will return with great knowledge and power if you survive. Also, when I say you are aware of the dark portals, I do not mean you can see them. You can only sense them. You will feel ice cold from walking by one. If the deepest part of your soul wishes to come across one, you will be attracted to it like a magnet. Now, I suppose you are enjoying your newly found knowledge, but you won't have it for long."

"Why not?" it sounded like a plea for mercy.

"I cannot have people knowing too much. What I just told you is far from common knowledge, and you are not worthy of superior knowledge. This means that I must kill you."

"PLEASE, NO, DON'T!!" the shriek made Erin's grip tighten on my sleeve.

"I apologize, but I must. That is the price that you pay for knowledge. I promise I will try not to drag it out too long."

There was a loud tear followed by a sharp, screeching noise. My eyes had finally started to adjust. I could see we were in an L-shaped room. We could not see the cannibals, and they couldn't see us. The powerful cannibal was tearing the other apart, and it was throwing the pieces onto our side of the room.

When each piece landed, it spewed blood and twitched. Then, it was frozen and unmoving. When the tearing noise finally stopped, a door was slammed. I leaned over to see what had happened, but the cannibal was gone and a portal shattered behind it.

"Are we safe now?" Erin asked.

"I think so," I whispered.

"Let's sort the gems," I had almost forgotten about them. Luckily, Erin remembered what all of them were for.

It was hard to sort them in the dark, but hopefully we were close enough. We put the emeralds in my bag, the sapphires in Erin's, and the rubies in And's. We decided to split the diamonds evenly among the three bags, just to be safe; and we each held one in our hand.

When I looked around, the room was filled with portals. All of them were different shapes and sizes, but they had the same gold-silver outline and bright, heated center. Some of them were the same as the mirror we had used to get here, but most of them were much different.

The circle-shaped portals had shimmery light moving around the edges, and the center was a whirlpool of light. The triangle ones had a very thin stream of light around the edges, and the corners were overwhelming.

The last one, I couldn't even describe as a specific shape. It looked like a paint splatter, and all of the shimmery light was swirled in with the heated center. The portal that we had used to get into the diamond mine was now small and narrow.

The only thing that could fit through it was a rat, but that would even be pushing your luck. We were not going to be returning to the mine anytime soon.

Erin's grip softened until it was nonexistent. She held the diamond tightly in her hand, and she began walking along the wall. Her footsteps were a soft, simple heartbeat, and it paused every time she reached a portal.

She would run her fingers along the edges of it, and then she brushed her hand against the center of it. Her hand never lingered when she brushed the center. It was like she was running her hand against a hot windowpane.

The heat felt good and comforting at first, but then it became too intense and started to burn your hand. When she had finished walking around the room, she came back to where I was standing.

"Figure anything out?" I sounded sarcastic, but I was still completely serious.

"Unfortunately, not much about where they lead to. Each one is probably different," she admitted, "But we are going to have to be careful about which portals we go through. The circle ones made me feel super dizzy and weak. The paint splatter ones made my vision all blurry and filled with dots. The triangular ones make you feel like needles are being pressed into your skin. Lastly, there are the rectangle ones. We know they're perfectly safe, so we should stick to them."

"Well, that's a start I guess," I tried to be optimistic, "Which one we going to go through?"

"I'm not sure, but I think we should wait a minute and rest here. There are more stars than I have ever seen before."

"What are stars?" I was so confused. I had no idea what she could possibly be talking about.

"Look up," she told me.

When I looked up, it was like nothing I had ever seen before. The usually black sky was filled with bright, little white dots. At first I thought of snowflakes, and I wondered if it was snowing; but all of them stayed where they were, and they lit up the sky.

"What the...," I trailed off.

"Aren't they beautiful?" she sounded as if she was in a trance.

"What are those things? Are they dangerous?" I began to worry that this was a roadblock. If so, I was completely unprepared for it.

"Don't be stupid; they're stars. They're how we get our light on the surface. They fill the universe, and they provide Earth and other planets with light. The most important star on Earth is called the Sun. Without the Sun, everyone would die," she rolled her eyes.

"Your light doesn't come from torches?" I had never heard of such a ridiculous thing in my life.

"It can, but it primarily comes from the Sun, and at night it comes from the other stars, too," she responded.

"How many stars exist?" I asked.

"Too many to count," she answered

"You said there are other planets?" I questioned.

"Yes, the universe, from what we know, is never ending. The numbers of things in it are infinite. It just goes on and on," she explained.

"How does a star give you light, I don't get it?" my head was filled with awe and confusion from my newly learned information.

"I'll explain it to you later, but for now let's just enjoy them," she ended the conversation.

We lied on our backs and gazed up at the stars. They were so beautiful, I almost forgot about everything that was important. Erin pointed out what she called constellations.

These were pictures made from imaginary lines connecting the stars. Many of them were recognized by something specific; for example, the mighty hunter Orion was found by finding three stars in a row. These stars represented his belt.

It would have been silent if I couldn't hear the sound of my heart beating. My eyes were frozen to the stars. I wondered if I would ever want to leave this place. It turned out to not be as hard as I thought it would be to leave.

On the other side of the room, there were voices again.

"What is this?" the first voice was like a bomb that had just been set off.

"It appears to be a dead cannibal," the answer was immediate and obvious.

"I know that, don't be an idiot. I meant, why is it here?" frustration filled each and every one of the words, "never mind about that, just go clean it up."

Feet shuffled towards us. I watched as pieces of the dead cannibal slowly disappeared. We were sitting still and waiting to be noticed. Finally, the creature began to move back to the other half of the room.

We slowly started to slide back towards the wall. My foot barely bumped a pebble. I thought nothing of it, until there was a small ding. It had hit the wall behind us.

"Lucky" for us, that wall was made out of metal. I squeezed the diamond in my hand, and I looked for a portal. We were going to need an escape route.

The creature spun around. Its giant yellow eyes scanned the room, and they stopped when they landed on us. It moved so fast, it was only a blur. When it stopped, it was face to face with us. So much for an escape plan...

"What are you two doing down here? Isn't it a little bit dangerous for a couple of kids to be roaming the maze alone?" Its sympathy sounded real, but we both knew that it was only a mask.

"We are doing quite fine, and if you don't mind we will be on our way," I wanted nothing more than to get away from that thing.

"Why don't you come with me? I'm sure you would find it much more enjoyable to travel this way. It would be a shame if anything happened to those pretty faces of yours," it ran its fingers along the outline of my face and moved the hair out of my eyes.

Its fingers felt cold and rough, like sandpaper rubbing against my face. I clenched my jaw. Its skin was thin and tight. It was a milky color, and beneath it there were black veins that swayed back and forth.

Its nose was almost nonexistent, and its ears were the same as a dog's. Its teeth were dull and uneven, and it reeked of death. I had never thought of death as a smell, but I knew that this was it.

It had a long, thin, emerald tail tightly coiled behind it. I shifted to one side. I hoped I could get away from the creature, but its tail slashed at my feet and pushed me back towards the wall.

"Don't think that you can get away that easily," the creature's voice was velvet, "You will be much better off if you just cooperate; and if you don't, I will call my majesty over. When she comes, you will have no choice but to come along. The more you fight, the more you will suffer later."

"What's taking you so long?" the creature that was in control growled from the other side of the room.

"It'll be just a minute," the creature in front of us sounded obedient and terrified at the same time, "I am sorry that it is taking this long, your majesty." If the other creature was the majesty, we were in trouble. I knew that we had to get out of there, but I had no idea how we were going to do it.

"You better be," the majesty groaned, "you know how I hate waiting."

"Yes, of course. I will try to hurry up," then, the creature in front of us lowered its voice, "come now or I can guarantee that you will suffer, and you will be disposed of when we are finished with you."

I never got to respond. It was looking into my eyes, and Erin took that brief moment to strike. She stabbed it in the heart, and it crumpled to the floor.

"Silly girl," it began to rise to its feet, "I am too powerful. You cannot kill me. You just made your life shorter and more miserable. I will make sure you scream for mercy," the creature cackled.

"I didn't need to kill you." Erin grabbed my hand and pulled me towards a portal so fast, we didn't get to hear a reply.

This portal was longer than the other had been. Before, we had practically just stepped through a wall and ended up in the next room. This time we were in the portal for at least a few minutes. The entire time, I was tense. All I could think of was where we were going to end up. If we ended up in the same room, we were dead meat.

Inside, the portal was different than I expected it to be. Last time, I hadn't paid attention. The trip was too short for me to take in my surroundings. This time, I could clearly see everything. It smelled like cleaning supplies, and I felt like I was walking through a cloud. Everything ahead of me was slightly blurry, and I couldn't see my own feet through the fog.

Everything felt soft and smooth against my skin, but it was like cotton candy. You can enjoy it for a second, but then it is gone. You barely remember it, but you have to get another bite. When we stepped out of the portal, there was a cloud of dust.

I waved my hands around to see where the portal had taken us, but the dust was so thick that I started coughing. When the dust finally thinned enough I could see my hands in front of my face.

They were covered in ash and dust. It looked like I had just escaped a burning building. I was completely black, and I couldn't stop coughing up ash and dust. My eyelashes were dusted with the black dust, and it kept falling into my eyes.

My eyes had finally stopped watering, and I turned around. The creature's face began to emerge from the portal. I struck at the portal with as much force as I could, but it didn't shatter. It seemed as if I had merely bumped into it or brushed it with my hand.

Erin and I locked eyes for a split second, and I knew that we were both thinking the same thing. We were thinking what any logical person would have thought: Run. We took off sprinting as fast as we could, and began jumping blindly through portals without turning back.

The sharp point of a jewel was digging into the palm of my hand, and my grip tightened with every step I took. I began to feel dizzy from going through so many portals. I started wondering if it was safe to go through them at all.

I didn't hear the creature behind us, so I slid the jewel in my hand back into my backpack. I took out a different one. Hopefully this one could shatter portals. I had to run faster than ever before to catch up with Erin.

When I finally had caught up with her, I felt like I was about to fall over. My throat was dry and I could barely breathe. My legs had gone numb, but now they were beginning to cramp. I knew we wouldn't make it much longer.

We were running down a hall filled with portals on both sides. Erin seemed determined to reach the end, but I didn't know what her reasoning was. I heard loud footsteps behind us. They told me we would never make it in time.

I caught hold of Erin's arm, and I pulled her through the nearest portal. Afterwards, I struck at it with the diamond. I threw all of my weight behind the blow, and it was worth it. I watched as the portal crumbled to the ground. The only thing left was a pile of glass.

I fell forward onto my knees, and I reached for my water. I drank nearly half of it. This moment would come back to haunt me. I didn't need that much water, but I couldn't stop drinking. The only thing I could hear was the sound of us breathing throughout the room.

The room was dark, so I couldn't see what was in it. I could only make out shapes in the shadows. I began to walk forward to get a closer look, but it turned out I didn't need to. When I walked, dust began floating up from the ground.

The floor was stained with blood. The room smelled like death, and the ceilings went on forever. Pockets of light were scattered across the walls, and they were framed with sharp pieces of metal. Human bones had been carelessly tossed around the room.

Across the room there was a portal. This was the only one in the room, but it still seemed too convenient. I couldn't help being skeptical. Anyone would have been if they were in my position.

CHAPTER XI
ERIN

The blood didn't scare me. The metallic smell of it somehow felt familiar. What did scare me were the bones. None of them were whole. There were just bits and pieces scattered around the room.

All of them were cleanly cut. None of them had sharp or jagged edges. I didn't know of anything that could cut so cleanly through human bones. More importantly, why would the murderer bother with destroying the bones? All they did was leave them behind.

"Why would anyone tear bones to pieces only to abandon them?" I thought aloud.

"I don't think it was a someone who did this," Alex reasoned.

"Well, like obviously someone couldn't have done this alone; what I'm confused about is why they would do it," I complained.

"I mean, I think it was a something," he explained.

"What kind of something?" I questioned.

"Look up," he spoke to me like I was an irrational little kid.

Above us, there were long, interlocked blades. The spaces between them were narrow. It was questionable whether or not a person would be able to fit through one of them. The blades were slowly lowering towards us, and my heart began to race.

They weren't moving towards us very fast, but we still wouldn't be able to make it to the portal in time. Still, I ran towards it. I could hear the sound of my heart beating and my feet pounding against the ground.

I felt like I was in my own little world. All that existed was me and the portal. Nothing else mattered. I had gotten used to the rhythm of my breath. My heartbeat was in synch with my feet. My body was its own symphony.

A hand on my shoulder pulled me out of my bubble. I spun around expecting to see a creature, but it was only Alex. His eyes were wild, and his hands were shaking. The blades were only yards above us. The portal was too far; we couldn't make it. Alex held his arms above his head as we waited for the blades to reach us.

"What are you doing?" I questioned him.

"Trust me, I have an idea," his eyes lit up. He knew what he was doing, and I was going to listen to him.

I held my hands above my head, too; but I still had no idea why. When the blades reached Alex's fingertips he wrapped his hands around them. He positioned his body beneath a gap in the blades, and slowly he pulled himself through it.

He was now standing on top of the blades. I could finally reach the blades. I wrapped my hands around them and pulled myself up. The edges bit into my hands, and I could feel blood flowing down my arms.

Alex knelt down and helped me pull myself on top of the blades. My hands and arms were sticky from my blood, but I barely noticed. Pain, blood, and death were all just a part of the maze's game. You couldn't avoid them, but they made you stronger. I was beginning to wonder if strength made you less of a person inside.

We kept walking towards the portal, and the blades eventually hit the floor. Once they did, it was time for round number two. A set of blades came out from opposite walls, and the space between them started to shrink.

My instincts took over, and I ran towards the blades in front of me. Running on blades was hard. I kept falling through the gaps and giving myself mini heart attacks. I finally reached the blades, and I started to climb.

I needed to get to the top before the sets of blades met each other. The gaps between the blades were too small to fit through, so this was my only option. When I grabbed the blade, I felt nothing more than a slight pinch. Finding places to put my hands and feet was easy, but my blood made everything slippery. I kept losing my footing and barely catching myself in time.

By the time I got to the top of the blades, I had plenty of leeway. I was able to start my descent before the blades even touched. When I looked up, another set of blades was coming down from the ceiling. If I hadn't thought to climb down, I could have been stuck doing this forever. The ceilings were endless, and so was the obstacle.

I finally reached the portal, and I leaned against the wall to steady myself while I waited for Alex. As soon as my back touched the cold stone, all of the blades disappeared. Alex fell the remaining distance to the ground. The drop wasn't too far, but he still limped over to me.

"What did you do?" he panted.

"I have no idea. I didn't mean to do that, I swear," I felt guilty.

"No worries, I'm just messing with you. Have a sense of humor," he teased.

"That's so mean," I laughed.

Alex raised his eyebrows as if to say, "What are you going to do about it?" and I hit him with the back of my hand. My palms were coated in blood, and I was exhausted.

My legs felt weak, and staying on my feet was painful. My adrenaline was gone, and all I wanted to do was sink to my knees. Alex looked just as bad. His face was pale and glistening with sweat.

He used his sleeve to clean off his face, and the muscles in his arms stood out like battle scars. They were there to show what he had been through. Most importantly, they were proof he was victorious. He survived, and that was the only thing that mattered here.

He had small cuts all over his legs and the inside of his arms. He must have been standing really close to the blades when he was climbing them. His hands were a bloody mess, and I couldn't see a piece of clean skin.

Now I was face-to-face with the portal. I felt myself shiver with excitement and worry. I couldn't wait to get out of this place, but I feared what we would be facing next. I was just about to step through the portal when I began to smell something clean and fresh. It filled my body, and I couldn't get enough of it.

I tried to fight the feelings at first, but eventually my body gave in. I lowered myself to the floor and closed my eyes. I imagined that I was in a meadow. Everything was peaceful, and I didn't have a care in the world.

My mouth began to water from hunger, and without thinking I dragged my bag in front of me. I emptied everything that was inside of it; I was a starving animal. I pawed through everything until I found what I was looking for: food.

There wasn't very much left. We would be able to get through another day or so, if we were lucky. I knew this wasn't the time and place to be eating what little we had left, but hunger gnawed at my stomach. My willpower caved, and I began to eat the only scraps we had left.

My imagination turned into daydreams, but they were different than ever before. I felt like I was being sucked into a world of nothing. I fought and I fought, but I couldn't pull myself out. I gave up suddenly, without even thinking. After that, it seemed like I would never be able to turn back.

I was in a dream that I couldn't wake up from. It was a great dream, but at the same time it felt wrong and evil. As every minute passed, I forgot more and more about why I was here. I began giving up and letting go of everything I had always said was important.

I didn't care about anything, and I laughed at how free I felt. I was on top of the world, and nothing was going to bring me down. I kept eating until there was nothing left. The food was gone, and so was I. I laid back and deeply inhaled the fresh, clean smell. I felt like I was being given a fresh start, but I was really just being careless.

Out of nowhere, the endorphins stopped. I no longer felt great or happy. My head was pounding, and I could barely pull myself up. I had to keep pausing and waiting for the pain to slow before I could keep moving. When I was sitting up, I had no idea where I was. Nothing looked familiar.

Everything was covered in a sheet of black. It was so dark that I couldn't see my own hand in front of my face. I panicked. I tried to stand up, but my feet were tied to the ground. I couldn't move. I had been tied up and pinned to the ground.

"Alex," I hissed. It took a few moments, but finally I heard a groan. He also said a few words he probably isn't proud of looking back on, but I'm not going to repeat them. The sound had come from slightly in front of me. I twisted and turned until I could move my foot back and forth. Although it was a long shot, I tried to kick forward. All that I connected with was air.

I stretched forward. I had to get his attention, but I didn't want to say anything. I had a feeling that we were being watched. My whole body was sore and it ached with every movement I made. Soon, I didn't care about the risks. Talking was my best option.

"Alex," I whispered; there was no response. I tried a few more times, but finally my temper was gone. I was trapped in a maze with no way out, I was hungry, And was dead, and all I could think about was how stupid I could possibly be. If I ever got home, I was never pulling another stunt like this. I snapped, "Alex, I know you're here so you better answer me before I break your jaw!"

Lights flicked on. I looked around. We were surrounded by cannibals.

"Oh, well, someone's getting feisty, how adorable," it sounded disgusting.

"Do not call me adorable." It was a stupid thing to say. We were tied up, exhausted, and greatly outnumbered; but what did it matter at this point. I knew I wasn't going to make it out of here alive. If I did, it would be a miracle.

"But you are," it responded, "I'm sure we will all enjoy having you as a little snack, but it's such a shame. You could have been useful to us."

It turned to Alex who was even more restrained than I was. The gas must have not been as effective on him. He looked bloody and beat; I smiled because he must have put up a good fight. I had no idea what it was doing until I was about to throw up.

It tilted Alex's head back and sank its teeth into the side of his neck. Alex tried to scream out in pain, but his mouth was tied, so only murmurs could escape. Its teeth were razor sharp as if they had been filed down with a knife.

Blood ran down the side of Alex's neck, and the creature licked his neck until no red was visible. I tried to turn away in disgust, but one of the other cannibals held my face in place. It wasn't going to let me stop watching now.

"You're next," it cackled, "Aren't you the slightest bit curious about what your friend's pain is like? You'll be joining him in no time."

I wasn't going to let them win; they wanted to scare me but I refused to show fear.

They wanted to hear me beg for mercy, but I wasn't going to. I kept my eyes fixed on Alex. The pain inside of him seemed to get worse and worse. His hands shook and his face was ghostly.

Finally it stopped and turned its head away from Alex. Two perfectly round punctures were left in the side of his neck, and streams of blood flowed out of them. It spilled onto his clothes and they began to stick to his skin.

"Don't just let the blood go to waste, someone needs to finish him off now that I'm full," it sounded amused. These things were worse than animals. All of them began to charge him, and although he could barely keep his eyes open, I could tell they were filled with worry.

I listened as pair after pair of teeth sank into his skin. The sound was sharp and it lingered in my ears, but I finally had a plan. They were all focused on Alex and had forgotten about me. I slipped out of the ropes tying me to the floor as silently as possible.

I slowly stood up, keeping my back against the wall to steady me. Then, I began to move forward. The exit was clear and I thought about leaving, but I wouldn't have been able to live with the guilt if I left Alex to die.

I hadn't been noticed, but that soon changed. The

cannibal who had already fed was watching the others and grinning, but that didn't stop it from seeing me. All of my instincts told me to run, but I wasn't going to lose someone else to a bunch of dirty cannibals.

There was going to be a fight, and this time I was not going to stand aside and let someone else do the work. I couldn't. Everything was on my shoulders and it was my responsibility to win.

It leapt at me with red eyes glowing due to fury. It gripped my shoulders and pushed me into the wall. My head flew back, and smashed into the wall. Images swam in my eyes and I had no way of telling what was real and what was not. My ears were ringing, and my knees shook.

"Oh, not so aggressive anymore, are you?" it cackled.

"I'm still strong enough to kill you," I growled.

I was face-to-face with it; I knew that I had nowhere to go. I couldn't run and I couldn't fight. I was left with one choice: I had to make a deal with the cannibal.

"What do you want?" I demanded.

"You're such a silly little girl. Your friend killed my father. I saw you hiding at the top of the webs. If I hadn't been so distracted, I would have gone and killed you. You were too weak to help your friend and he died, but the two of you still have each other. I have nothing left. One of you can go if the other agrees to come with us. What awaits you will not be pleasant, and neither of you will be safe. You will have to be just as miserable as me. Both of you will know what pain actually is."

"I'll do it," I needed to come up with an escape plan

fast. If I didn't, something bad was certain to happen, "just let Alex go."

"Halt," it commanded. All of the others instantly turned to face it. Their faces were covered in blood, and their eyes were glowing from recently feeding. They were strong, but the endorphins hadn't worn off enough for them to be smart. This was my chance.

I pushed my way through them and released Alex before any of them knew what I was doing. There was a narrow door. Getting through it with Alex was going to be a challenge. He had lost so much blood, it was shocking that he wasn't dead yet. But he would be if I didn't get him treated soon.

His face was drained. No traces of color were left behind. Teeth marks were scattered across his body, and they were still dripping the little blood he had left. His eyes were bloodshot and he was nearly unconscious. The only sign that he was still alive was his rough breathing and infrequent heartbeat.

They were all staring at me, fascinated with my reaction. Some looked ashamed, but most of them looked like they thought we deserved it. None of them had blank expressions. Alex had lost enough blood that I could hold him in my arms. He was still and fragile; I had never seen him look so vulnerable before. One of the cannibals looked towards me and nodded its head. I needed no other signal before I was out the door.

I could barely walk, and putting one foot in front of the other was a challenge. My head pounded, and the path in front of me seemed to sway back and forth. I kept one arm against the wall; I was worried that I would fall over the edge if I didn't.

Finally I spotted a hole in the bottom of the wall. I set Alex on the ground and used my entire body weight to push him through. Then I dropped to my knees and crawled through the opening. It was one of those rare moments when I was grateful to be smaller than most people.

Fortunately, the ceiling was higher inside. I could stand if I leaned forward, and I was able to lean Alex against a wall. We were safe, but now I had an entirely new problem on my hands. I had no idea where to start on bandaging his wounds; he and And had always been the ones to deal with that kind of thing.

I did my best to remember the many times we had gotten hurt before now, and tried to copy what they had done. I couldn't make anything work, so I decided to do whatever looked like it would help. In the end my work was a complete mess, but none of his blood was leaking out anymore.

I thought that he would have had at least some change by now, and I was right; but the change was for the worst. His heartbeats were becoming further and further apart, and with every minute his breathing slowed.

Once again I had to make a decision. An idea formed in my head, but it was the last thing I would ever want to do. I tried to come up with something else, but eventually my time ran out. I grabbed hold of the knife and took a long deep breath. Once I did this, there was no turning back.

I closed my eyes in terror of what I was about to do, and I slowly lowered the knife. It pierced the top layer of my skin and pain flamed within me. I pushed down harder. It took everything I had not to stop or scream out in pain.

I kept going until there was a long, jagged gash along my arm. Then, I pulled out one of the empty water containers and held it against the cut. I tilted my arm to allow my blood to flow into it. There was a thin, uneven stream slowly filling the container.

The pain never stopped, it only worsened. The stream started to slow until only drops were left. My hands were shaking, and my arm was throbbing. Still, there wasn't enough blood. I had to make the gash deeper and longer.

I wanted to close my eyes like I had before, but I had to make sure I didn't kill myself. The knife dug into my arm and fuel was added to the fire. In this case, the fire was my pain. It was almost unbearable at this point. The cuts I made now were deep. I was practically looking death in the eye.

I poured more blood into the container. This time, it came out in a thick, even stream. I never imagined that I would be doing this. I didn't even know if it would work. When the container was filled to the top, I set it on the ground and quickly tied a piece of bandage around the cut.

The bandage was soaked in seconds, but that didn't matter right now. Alex was more important. I dragged myself towards him and peeled back one of his bandages. The cut below was deep, but not deep enough.

"I'm sorry," I whispered in his ear. He did nothing

in response which told me my time was almost gone. With the knife I sliced further down into his skin. Then, I took the container and started pouring my blood into his body.

A thin, even stream of blood flowed into him. I couldn't believe the amount of blood he had lost. His body absorbed the blood like a desert floor.

I poured until the container was empty. I tossed it aside and reached up to feel his pulse. It was still slow, but it was steadier than it had been before. I wanted to give him more blood, but I wasn't even sure if it had helped.

All I could do now was wait. Wait for him to die. Wait for him to live. Wait.

I didn't even notice I had fallen asleep until I woke up. Immediately I turned to check on Alex. He was pale, but he wasn't a ghost like he had been yesterday. I almost cried with relief.

I reached up to feel his pulse, and I was overjoyed. It might have been slow, but it was even and steady. He never missed a beat. When I took my hand away, his eyes shot open. He was staring at me with sad, miserable eyes. It wasn't right. His eyes were meant to be full of hope and faith.

He reached out and slowly pulled me towards him. His hands were strong and careful, exactly the way I remembered them. I smiled a little. It was only a matter of time until things would be back to normal. I wasn't going to lose someone else today.

"I know what you did for me," he whispered in my ear. My mind instantly flashed back to what I had done. I knew then that my blood had saved him. He continued,

"I'm grateful but you shouldn't have done it. You shouldn't risk your life for me like that."

"I had to," I was coming dangerously close to my breaking point. He didn't understand why I had saved him, and I didn't want to explain. The look on his face told me I didn't have a choice, "After And was gone," I started, "I didn't know if I had the strength to go on any longer. I let him die for me. I wasn't going to let you join him."

"And made his own decisions; you can't blame yourself for what happened," he replied.

"Then why do I blame myself? I can never stop thinking about that moment! Everything reminds me of it. I have no way to escape!" That was all it took. I reached my breaking point. Tears flooded my face and left a salty taste in my mouth. I wanted to be strong. I had never been so weak before.

Alex didn't say anything. He just held me in his arms like he was my big brother, and I was his little sister who had gotten hurt. Finally, Alex found the right words, but they were the last thing I had ever expected him to say.

"And loved you. Whenever we were between shifts, he would go on and on about you. He didn't think he would ever meet a person like you. I don't want you to take this the wrong way, but he came because of you. He wanted to make sure you were taken care of and kept safe. He died for someone he loved. It was the best way for him to show you how much he cared."

My mouth went dry. I had no idea what to say. I loved And as more than family but I was never certain he loved me back in the same way. I was convinced that he was here because of Kate. I had missed it. I had missed my chance at love because I convinced myself that he wanted someone else and he could never love me as more than a sister.

My tears came harder and harder. My face was a hurricane. On the outside, I looked like a mess. On the inside, everything was being torn apart. Alex comforted me, but I would have given anything to have And's arms around me instead.

It was clear that I shouldn't have been such a coward. I couldn't have been more frustrated with myself, but I was grateful that Alex had told me. I felt satisfaction knowing that I was more than a sister to And.

I leaned my head back against Alex's chest, and I continued to cry until my eyes were dry and my face was drenched. When I was finished drying my face, I crawled back through the narrow opening that we had used to get here.

Alex was right behind me, and we were greeted with chaos. Battle cries filled the air and dead bodies littered the ground. They had been torn to pieces which had been scattered everywhere. The distinct smell of blood lingered in the air.

I recognized the cannibal who had been the leader. Just looking at his red eyes made me want to kill him. I probably would have if he wasn't already dead.

Then I saw the cannibal who had nodded at me to leave. It was the only cannibal I had ever seen that showed any sort of sympathy. I wondered if it still had a trace of being human left inside. And if it did, could it have been saved and reverted back to its human state?

Its eyes were black. It stood out among the red ones like an ocean in the desert. It was the only one that didn't feed on Alex. I was willing to bet that it was the first one killed. It had to have been weak from not eating.

Guilt swelled in my chest, and I turned away from the scene. I felt like a terrible person for feeling upset over their deaths. What kind of person could take pity on heartless creatures who tried to kill her best friend?

Alex's eyes were glued to the scene, and I practically had to pull him away. He acted like a robot with no emotion. He walked with me, but he kept staring off into space.

"Are you alright?" I asked when we turned the corner.

"I guess. It's just weird looking at those things that nearly killed me yesterday," he tried to make it seem like it wasn't a big deal, but I knew he wasn't taking it lightly.

"I can't believe they're still fighting," I was genuinely shocked that there hadn't been a winning side yet.

"When cannibals fight, there is no winning side," Alex explained, "they fight until only one of them is left. They don't trust each other in battle. Friends turn on each other every day. It's every creature for itself."

"Oh," every time I learned new information about the cannibals, I felt more and more disgusted by their repulsive ways.

"We should go while they're still distracted," the look on Alex's face said that he wanted to wait and see what happened, but he knew I was afraid. He didn't want me to be uncomfortable after I had just saved his life.

I looked down at my arm for the first time today. The cut was jagged, and my skin was rough. The cut was slightly raised, and dried blood caked my arm. I brushed off the little flecks as we walked. When Alex noticed he pulled out one of the water containers to clean it for me. It was empty, and so were all the others. We had no water or food left.

I felt myself go tense, and we both stared at each other. It seemed like we had more than enough food when we left. It didn't seem possible for us to go through it all so quickly. This was a problem we hadn't anticipated.

No food and no water. This was about to become a much more interesting adventure.

CHAPTER XII
ALEX

My worst nightmares were coming true. We were stuck in the maze. We had been captured and nearly killed by cannibals. Our physical condition was terrible, and now we had no water or food left. Although I would never admit it to Erin, I was scared.

Being captured was terrifying. When they fed off of me, I almost didn't want them to stop. It was nice to forget about the world for a little while, and dying seemed like an easy way to solve my problems. The pain was intense, but I couldn't get enough. It felt pure, and for once, there were no strings attached.

If Erin hadn't stopped them, no one would have. I would be dead because I gave up. Dying for a greater cause is one thing, but I almost died from selfishness. To me, when I didn't fight, I may as well have been the one slitting my own throat.

I knew that I couldn't keep worrying about the past. There was nothing I could do about it now. I had to focus on what was important right now, and that was food. If we didn't find something to eat, we were going to die. There was no question about it.

We kept walking along the wall until we returned to the type of paths we were used to. Here, there were walls on both sides, and they were covered in vines. We didn't want to stop walking until we had found food. I had a feeling we would be walking for a while.

That day marked four days. I knew lack of food would ultimately catch up to us, but I didn't think it would affect us as much as it did. We had been walking nonstop, and I could feel my body slowly deteriorating. Fortunately, we didn't run into any more roadblocks or cannibals. If we had, we wouldn't have stood a chance.

My stomach growled, and pain shot through it. Hunger was taking over my body, and Erin was affected even more. She was so much smaller than me, and every day she seemed to get skinnier. I worried that she would snap in half if she fell down.

The vines taunted me, and I wanted to eat one of them so badly. Multiple times a day, I would start walking towards them with my hands reaching out; but every time, I heard And's voice echoing in my head. They weren't safe. It had to be a trap.

Another day went by, and I was becoming desperate. I couldn't let Erin test the vines to see if they were safe, so I was left with one option. I pulled a vine off of the wall and bit into it.

A thick bitter liquid flowed down my throat and into my stomach. My hunger was beginning to fade, but something about the vine didn't seem safe. I was pretty sure I had just fallen into a trap.

The liquid was thick and sticky. At first, I had no problem forcing it down my throat, but then it began to suffocate me. It felt like someone was pouring cement into my body. If I died, this would be a slow and dreadful death.

Death is scary to everyone, but I always knew that I wanted to go fast. A quick, simple death seemed so much better than a drawn out one. I was about to face one of my deepest fears. Within moments, I blacked out.

I didn't know I was falling until my head hit something hard. After that, everything was black. I looked around and saw myself back home. My family was gathered around the table. Everyone was there, except for me.

And and Erin were sitting side-by-side. The way that they looked at each other made my body fill with envy and longing. Their eyes sparkled, and they were able to communicate by just looking at one another.

No one noticed me there. I tried to talk to all of them, but I was a ghost. My life was over. Now, I was nothing more than a translucent person. I had no shadow, and I was invisible to the living.

Pain was all that I felt. I had always believed that once you died, you would go to another place — but here I was. I was stuck in the place I knew better than anywhere else. I was supposed to have no questions, but instead I was overwhelmed with them.

I wanted to know how And was still alive. I had seen his dead body, unmoving and still. As much as it pained me to admit it, there was no way Erin could have survived on her own. She had no provisions left, and lack of food and sleep had left her weaker than ever.

Then the room dissolved, and I was standing in an endless hallway with Kate. She could see me, but only because she was dead, too. The more I looked around, the more figures I could recognize. They were all people I had known and loved.

Kate was the first one to speak to me, "Alex," she whispered, "it's been forever, but I see you have found your way here."

"What exactly is here?" I questioned.

"You're in the land of the dead," she explained, "I imagine that you have already been able to see your family for the last time. Now you have been sent here to wait."

"Wait for what?" I questioned.

"To be judged," she acted like it was a ridiculous question, "After you die, you need to be judged. That's how it's determined if you will stay in this world, or if you will be ready to move on. If you move on, you will be able to decide who you want to watch over. You can pick one person, and then you will spend the rest of their life watching over them. When they die, you are free to do whatever you want."

"Was anyone watching over me?" I asked.

"Yes," she hesitated, "but that is not information that I can tell you. The only person who can reveal that information to you is the person who was watching over you. However, I can tell you that their voice talked to you in times of need."

"How long do I have to wait here?" I wondered aloud.

"It all depends on how quickly the trials ahead of you go. Sometimes they are only a matter of minutes, but other times they can take years upon years. Don't worry though; time goes by faster when you're dead," she gave me a half smile.

I looked down the hallway and saw people everywhere. The hallway went on so far I couldn't see the end. The entire place glowed with a warm, gold light, similar to the one I saw in myself when I was with my family.

I caught pieces of conversations, and they all made things seem worse. People were complaining about how they had been waiting for hundreds of years, and how boring it was to be here.

I turned back to Kate, "How did you die?"

"Don't you already know that?" she looked at me cryptically.

"All I know is that you never came out of maze. I don't know why," I admitted.

"When And and I went into the maze, neither of us thought that the dangers were real. We had just assumed that they were rumors. Anyway, I got separated from And. I didn't think anything of it, and I assumed it would be fun to try and find each other," she sighed and continued, "I saw cannibals, and I screamed. They hadn't noticed me yet, but they did then. They hadn't fed in days, and all of them swarmed me. The venom stopped me from fighting, and I was even more scared when I realized that I liked it. They thought I was dead when they left me, but I was barely alive. When And found me I was almost dead. He tried to take care of me but in the end, it wasn't enough. I died in his arms. After that, he swore that he would never let the maze kill another person he loved."

"I'm so sorry," I had no idea what else to say.

"It's okay," she replied, "when I got here, I met the person who was watching over you. I made them promise to give me updates on And every day. At first they were hard to hear because he was grieving over my death; but eventually he found hope again. That was when he met Erin. Since then, I haven't asked for any more reports. I knew that he was happy, so I was finally able to let him go."

"And died; he should be here. Where is he?" I frantically began scanning the room.

"He's not dead. He landed on a ledge, but he was so far down that you couldn't hear him. He was taken by the cannibals, and now he is with Erin's sister. I don't know why he's being held prisoner with her, but there has to be a reason. They don't play with their food," she shook her head.

"Thank you, Kate. Thank you so much. I have been so worried that he was dead, but you gave me hope again. How can I ever repay you?" I was relieved beyond belief to learn I hadn't lost my brother...at least not yet.

"If you get sent back into the world, it means that

you have unfinished business. If that happens to you, please promise me something," she looked me dead in the eye.

"Anything," I told her.

"Promise me that you will do whatever it takes to keep And and Erin together. Even if I'm sent back and I try to mess things up, don't let it happen," she begged.

"I promise, but how do you know that you are not the one who belongs with him?" I knew I couldn't mess with my brother's love life unless Kate truly knew what she was talking about.

"He never thought of me as anything more than a friend. He tried to have feelings for me, but fake love never works. If things had been real, he wouldn't have been able to move past my death or fall for Erin," she looked as though she was on the brink of tears.

"Why do you still have hope then?" I was utterly confused.

"After seeing And and Erin together, I know that true love does exist. I want to find it for myself. That's another reason you have to keep me from messing with the balance of things," she regained control of her emotions and no longer seemed so sad.

"If it's true then I don't know if you even could break it," I commented.

"Everything that is made can be broken. In the end, both of them would be heartbroken. They wouldn't heal, but they would never get back together because as much as they want each other, they want one another to be happy," she explained.

"Why do you need me to stop you? I mean, you seem pretty set in stone about what you think, so couldn't you stop yourself?" I desperately wanted to change her mind about our deal and protect myself from ending up in the middle of a complicated love triangle.

"I'm afraid it isn't that easy," she started, "if you are sent back into the real world, you won't remember anything you saw here. The only things you will remember are the promises you made, and if you are reborn, you will not remember anything about your past life."

"Is it common for people to come back?" I needed to know.

"Most people are reborn at least once. Each time you come back, you have to relearn everything. But relearning things becomes easier and easier with every lifetime," she told me.

"How do you know so much about the land of the dead and balance of the universe?" I had no idea how someone so young could be so wise.

"I ask a lot of questions, much like you do. You probably know more than a lot of people here already. Some people have been here for years, and they still have no idea where they are," her response only added to my confusion.

"Is that a good thing?" I bit my lip hoping I hadn't just asked a stupid question.

"It all depends," she began, "some people say that they would prefer not to know anything so that they can feel like they have total freedom. Other people dedicate their entire existence to the pursuit of knowledge."

"What do you mean? Is there a point where your existence completely fades and you become nothing?" my head was spinning.

"Yes. Once you have truly nothing left to exist for, you fade away. It has only happened to a few people before, and no one knows what happened or where they went. They could have just fallen off of the grid for all we know — but we have to be suspicious because they are the oldest people we know of," she lowered her voice in a way that made me wonder if I wasn't supposed to know this information.

"How long have they existed?" I was certain my eyes were wide with awe.

"They had been alive since the start of the first universe," her answer was simple yet complex at the same time.

"There's more than one universe?" I couldn't believe that I didn't know something so big.

"Too many to count. It would take billions of years traveling at the speed of light to reach the next universe. That's where portals come in. All of them exist in the maze because it is a very central place. Once you are done watching over someone, most people travel throughout the different universes," Kate tried her best to make all the bits and pieces in my head come together.

"Has anyone ever come back to life after coming to the land of the dead, without going through the whole judging process?" I prayed the answer would be yes.

"There have been a few cases where people were frozen to death, and they were able to be brought back to life. However, without ice or some other substance that preserves things, it is impossible to return to your old life without a trial. Those cases are the hardest because when people come back, the judges prefer that they are born into a new life," she nearly crushed the small piece of hope I had left.

"Do they remember being here?" I asked.
"Yes, but they all think that it was just a dream they had while they were unconscious," she shrugged.

I had no questions left to ask. I couldn't come back to life without a trial, and that could take me millions of years to reach. I had to accept the fact that I was dead.

Gold dust rose from the floor and began swirling around me. I couldn't see anything, and judging from the muffled oohhhs and ahhhs I heard, I assumed this wasn't something that happened every day.

"What's happening?" I screamed.

"You're being summoned by the judges, good luck!" Kate replied.

I had no idea what she meant. Why would they summon me? There was no way that it was my turn for a trial, I had only been here for a matter of minutes.

When the gold dust cleared, I was standing in a room made entirely out of amber. There were carvings along every surface; they looked like maps with stories hidden within them.

Grand arches were everywhere, and there was a wide, gold sheet in the center of the room. In front of it, judges sat in a row at a long, grand table. In total there were six of them. The one in the center was the first one to speak.

"This is not something that we usually do," she stated, "Within the entire existence of the land of the dead, we have only summoned one other person. Can you guess who it was?"

"Kate?" I guessed. There was no other explanation that seemed logical. She seemed to know about everything that was happening.

"Yes. And what do the two of you have in common?" she tilted her head and stared into my eyes while she waited for my response.

"We are both victims of the maze," the words left my mouth before I had even thought of them.

"Yes. Another unique thing about the two of you is that you are the only people who have died a courageous death on your first life," she added.

"That was my first life?" I blurted in surprise.

"Yes, and it is a life that we would like you to return to. You are not entirely dead; your heart is still beating. You have only come here because your mind has died. However, your body is starting to die as well. Therefore, for the first time ever, we are going to save someone," she kept her voice steady and free of emotion.

"Why save me?" I wanted to know what about my life was special enough to change everything.

"You are the only one who can stop them," she said coldly.

"Who are 'them'?" I was tired of everyone assuming I knew more than I did.

"I'm afraid that I can't tell you that, but you need to

keep Erin safe. Find And and Annie. Also, save Ria if you can. All of you play an important part in what is about to come. It doesn't only affect people on Earth, but everyone in existence," she directed me.

"I will," I answered. I desperately wanted to know more, but her pursed lips told me that this conversation was over.

"Everything happens for a reason," she reminded me.

I had no time to ask what that meant because as soon as I had come there, I left. When I returned to my body, Erin was leaning over me and feeling my pulse. Tears were running down her face and leaving her dark hair damp.

She was talking quietly to herself, "Please, Alex, you can't die like this. Not here. Not now. Please."

I felt like someone had placed silver disks over my eyes because everything had a silver glow around it. It was like when you wake yourself up from a dream. A dream.

Was that a dream that I had just had? Was I really dead? What now? What was the important thing that I was supposed to do? A million questions filled my head, but all that I cared about was what they meant by "everything happens for a reason."

I had always believed that, but I had no idea what to make of this. I still didn't even know if it was a dream or if it was real. I knew that this was stupid; I should just forget about it. I pushed it to the back of my head and fought against it when it tried to come forward.

I forced my eyes fully open, and I slid my hand

over Erin's.

"I thought you were dead," she was still choking on her own tears, "never scare me like that again. I would rather die of starvation than be alone."

"I'll try not to," I tried to smile, but my throat felt tight so it ended up only being a half smile.

"Are you okay? Is there anything you need?" she was still concerned.

"I'm fine," I reassured her. I started to sit up, but I wasn't strong enough to do it by myself. Erin helped me, and then I leaned back against the wall. My head was pounding, and it felt like my insides were jumping up and down on a trampoline.

"I hate to do this to you," she began, "but we still need to find food."

"I figured that would still be an issue," I wasn't hungry anymore, but I had to remember that I had just eaten a vine that caused me to drift towards the line between life and death.

"Where should we start?" she was relying on me to take care of her, and I wasn't going to let her down.

I tried to think, but nothing seemed reasonable. Then it happened. I heard a voice in my head. It told me to go to the corner and run my knife along the edge. It seemed like a ridiculous idea — but if my trip had been real, then this was the person watching over me. I had nothing to lose, so I listened.

I refused to have help standing up, so I had to claw at the wall. I felt like a clawless cat trying to climb a tree. When I finally got up, I kept both hands on the wall, and I didn't dare lift my feet off of the ground.

I slid to the corner and held my knife in the palm of my hand. I wrapped my fingers around it, and I slowly slid it along the cement that bonded the walls together. Layers began to fall off, and each one was a different color.

When I finally reached the last layer, the walls split apart and revealed a small room. It was full of supplies. I heard Erin gasp behind me.

"Why didn't you do that sooner?" she sounded excited, but hints of anger and confusion lingered in her words.

"I didn't know it existed," I was just as shocked as she was.

"Then why did you decide to try that? What made you think it would work?" her confused expression was turning into excitement.

I weighed my options. I could tell her the truth, but then I would have to tell her the whole story about what had happened. I could lie, but I didn't want to run the risk of her finding out and getting mad at me.

"Promise, that you won't think I'm insane?" I exhaled.

"After everything that has happened, I don't know what insane is anymore; but yes, I won't judge you or anything," she said.

"I died." I didn't know how else to start it, but judging from the look on her face I should have done it another way. "I went to the land of the dead, and they told me that some people have someone who has died watching over them. My first thought was And, but they told me he's still alive. They brought me back to life because I have an important role to play, but they did not tell me any specifics. All they said was: if I hear a voice in my head, it is the person watching over me, and I should listen. Then they said, 'Everything happens for a reason,' and after that, I was back here." The words flew from my mouth, and half of them probably made no sense to her.

"Are you sure that it wasn't just a dream? Your pulse was weak, but it never stopped," she narrowed her eyes and bit her lip.

"You go to the land of the dead once your mind is dead. The rest of you dies later on. I know all this sounds crazy. I did not even believe it myself until, well, this happened," I admitted, gesturing towards the supply room.

"Well, this seems way too perfectly timed to be a coincidence," she observed, "I think that it might have been real, or a dream. But the only thing that's actually important is this was meant to happen. So we shouldn't over think things."

"I agree," a sense of relief washed over me. I hated being asked questions that I didn't know the answer to.

"Now, I don't know about you but I'm starving. Let's eat and repack so we can get going before any cannibals show up," she seemed to have sensed my discomfort and decided to change the conversation.

As I began to enter the room, the voice inside of my head began to speak again, "Don't take more than you can carry. There will be another stash in a few days' walk. Also, I know that you are wondering how I knew about this. I was one of the mappers of the maze. The stopping points can only be entered by chosen ones, so remember these are not only places to refill on supplies. They can be used as safe houses as well. No cannibals can enter."

I kept trying to ask questions, but the voice only ignored me. I felt like it wanted me to know as little as possible about what was happening and who he was. I wasn't even positive if it was a 'he.' I tried to remember what Kate had said, but those memories were blocked. I couldn't reach them no matter how hard I tried.

The provisions room was never ending. When we left, both of us had full stomachs and a week's supply of food. I thought about only bringing a few days' worth of food like the voice had instructed, but I wasn't going to take any chances. Out here, you never knew what was going to happen.

"Have you found out any new information?" Erin asked.

"What do you mean?" I replied.

"You keep talking to yourself and asking questions. I figured you were trying to communicate with the voice in your head," she shrugged.

"I was, but it won't answer back. For now, we are being left in the dark," it annoyed me that the voice seemed to think I didn't have the right to know what was happening inside of my own mind.

"I guess I don't really mind that, as long as we're not starving," she laughed.

"Oh, yes," I joked, "food is definitely the most important thing."

"Priorities, my friend, priorities," she said sweetly.

"Do you think that And is still alive?" this definitely wasn't the time to bring up something serious. We had just started to loosen up for the first time in a while, but my mind couldn't relax until I had an answer.

"Honestly, I'm not sure," she sighed, "all we can do is hope that he is. If not, he died like a hero and is in a better place now."

"I hope you're right; I haven't been able to stop thinking about what happened," I knew deep inside that Erin didn't have the answers I wanted, but it still disappointed me to have her confirm it.

"Don't let this slow you down or anything. If he's still alive, then we should be speeding up and trying to find him as soon as possible. We have three people to rescue now, so there's no time to waste," she tried to encourage me.

"I'll try, and in the meantime let's hope you don't start hearing a voice. I don't think either of us would ever be sane again if that happened," I wanted our conversation to return to the silly light-hearted one.

"Did you already forget?" she fake-gasped, "Food is my best friend. It is the most essential thing to me. Being sane isn't even close to as important as having a full stomach."

I felt relieved that I hadn't just ruined our whole conversation, but I knew that things were going to change now. The voice had added a new variable, and it was going to change everything. I still hadn't decided if it was a good thing or a bad thing, but hopefully the answer wasn't very far away.

CHAPTER XIII
ERIN

I never knew so many bizarre things could happen to a person in such a short amount of time. Alex had almost died, or maybe he had, but either way it was creepy. He started hearing a voice; and then all of a sudden, he knew where to find supplies. It just didn't seem right.

I was afraid that he might be going crazy, but I didn't have the strength to tell him. Maybe it was something to do with eating the vines. I had no idea what was happening anymore. My whole life felt like some sick joke, but I wouldn't have changed a thing. For once, my life was exciting.

There was a chance that Alex had in fact died and gone to some sort of in-between life. Alex was either going crazy, or there were some sort of higher beings controlling the world. I wasn't sure if I wanted to know what was happening, but I would do anything to find the answer.

I needed to know how someone could talk to Alex through his head and how powerful these voices really were. Did they have the power to use us as pawns in their own little game? Lastly, Alex believed he was meant to play an important role in the future because he was special enough to be saved when it had never been done before.

He was told that we were all part of some quest to kill evil. This was the kind of thing I had always daydreamed about growing up — and I still did sometimes in the maze, but now it was actually happening. I didn't know if I was ready to be a hero.

For now, I was just trying to stay positive and make things very light-hearted. As unsure as I was about taking food and supplies from the secret room, I did. I wanted Alex to think that I trusted and supported him. He thought everything that had happened was as real as the floor beneath our feet.

For the first time, Alex led us through the maze's twists and turns with confidence radiating off of him. He never hesitated to take a turn or a portal. His concentration was immense. I knew that he had to be listening to the voice.

For now, I had no complaints about it, but the voice seemed to be taking over him. I didn't like it, and something seemed wrong about it. The more he listened to it, the more he transformed into someone else.

I thought that he was being possessed, and I had to stop it. He trusted people too easily, without understanding that you have to be careful about whom you trust. So far, I didn't think he was making a very good decision.

I had seen many prisoners in my lifetime, so I knew when I shouldn't trust someone. There were dead giveaways like: wild eyes, uneasiness, and constantly looking over your shoulder to see if you were being watched or followed.

Most people can't tell when a person isn't trustworthy because they don't know what to look for but once you know, you can never forget. I would have been much more comfortable if I could actually see this person. Even listening to them would have made me feel better, but I was in the dark.

It took a while for me to build up enough courage to ask, "Do you even know where you're going?"

"Of course I do!" he snapped. This was definitely not like him.

"Maybe we should take a break; we've been covering a lot of ground in the past few hours," I suggested.

"We will take break when I say we take a break, now keep moving. We are on a mission, and I intend to accomplish it," he growled. The sound of his voice wasn't even the same anymore.

"You are SO NOT the boss of me, so do not talk to me like that. I will do what I want whether you like it or not, so deal with it," I challenged him.

"Actually, I will talk to you how I want to. If it was not for me, you would be lying dead from starvation a few miles back," he responded.

"I have saved your life plenty of times," I countered.

"Do I look like I care?" he scoffed.

"You should stop listening to that voice, and start

using your own head. Can't you see that it's taking over you? You're being possessed. I don't care how great you think it is, it's evil and it's not trying to help us," I wasn't going to give up until I had convinced him that he was wrong.

"Don't you dare insult the voice; and while you're at it, why don't you stop being an ungrateful little brat? We need it. Just accept that for once in your life, you are wrong. Not all of us can be right all the time; so maybe it's good that you're getting a chance to see what other people feel like all the time," he sounded exactly how I imagined a possessed person would.

His face was bright red, and he was sweating. The argument was making him furious, and he was beginning to enter his breaking point. Any normal person would have just shut up and gone along with things, but his eyes told me not to. I needed to keep pushing him. He needed to fall.

His eyes were crazed-looking, and they danced back and forth across the room. He wasn't just angry, he was nervous about something. There was a red ring around his irises that kept changing size and shade.

One second, it would look nearly gone. He would be calm. Next thing I knew, it would be dark and thick. He would look like he was ready to rip my head off. I was playing a game with death, but it was an irresistible one, and I wasn't going to lose.

"I'll stop acting like a brat when you stop being an idiot. And yeah, most people would be grateful or whatever for being saved from starvation; but I would rather be dead than be here with you right now." I didn't even get a chance to finish before his hand connected with my face.

I had been watching him the entire time I was talking. The Alex I knew was strong and fast, but he didn't know how to use the element of surprise. I hadn't even seen his hand leave his side. It was a blur as it shot through the air. This was not him.

My face felt like flames were being poured onto it. It burned, and the feeling wasn't something that only lasts for a few seconds. This pain didn't stop. Before I had even touched it, I could feel heat radiating from my skin.

My hand felt cool, and I could feel a bump beginning to form on my cheek in the shape of a handprint. I could only imagine what it was going to look like. I envisioned myself lobster- red where the handprint was and white as a ghost everywhere else from shock.

His eyes narrowed at me, "Is there anything else you would like to say?"

"There are a lot of things that I would like to say, but it doesn't mean that I should say them aloud," I grumbled.

"Finally, you're learning. Now come, and I expect to hear nothing but silence as you do." He had his head slightly tilted, and his smile emphasized the size of his canine-like teeth.

A shiver danced down my spine, but this time I went without complaining. I had learned my lesson, at least for now. New plans were already beginning to form inside of my head, but I wasn't sure how I was going to be able to accomplish any of them.

Our pace was brisk, and I struggled to keep up most of the time. By now we had probably traveled many miles from the supply area. Finally, Alex announced that he would allow us to have a five hour break for sleeping and eating.

"Who's going to take the first watch?" I asked.

"No one," he laughed to himself like I was an idiot, "We will both take a break, and then we will continue on. Taking watches wastes time, and I don't think anyone or anything will bother us."

I woke up to screaming. At first, I was scared that Alex was yelling at me; but then I realized that he was turned the other way. I wasn't tired, so I knew I had been asleep for more than five hours. I also knew this meant Alex wasn't being a drill sergeant anymore.

I instantly felt calmer, but the high-pitched screech put me back on edge. I didn't see anything anywhere. I had to be imagining it, or this was a dream. I tried to wake myself up. I forced my eyes open and closed over and over again, but it didn't work because I was awake.

Alex was still listening to the voice, and it was triggering the strongest emotions it could find. First, there was anger. Now, it was fear. I didn't want to find out what was going to happen next, but I did want to finish placing the pieces of the puzzle.

I ran over to Alex and placed my hands on his shoulders. His body went rigid, and he spun around on his heel. His face was full of fear. His eyes were wide, and his palms glistened with sweat. He kept his hand close to his knife as if he was expecting an attack.

"Alex," I said softly. I didn't want to scare him. It was like trying to get a stray puppy to come over to you. He was completely tuned out, so slowly I raised my voice until he finally heard.

"What?" he asked. His eyes were darting back and forth, sweeping the room for any potential danger.

"There is nothing to be afraid of," I reassured him, "you need to calm down or you're going to make yourself sick."

"You're wrong," he insisted, "I heard it. I saw it. There was a cannibal here, and then it vanished into thin air. It's going to be back any minute, and we have to be ready for when it attacks." His shaking hand was inching closer and closer to the knife.

"Stop!" I yelled and grabbed his hand. "You can't keep listening to the voice; please just ignore it. It's wrong! You can't let it keep controlling you."

When I looked into his eyes, I saw the red ring starting to fade. I was starting to reach him, and he was fighting against the voice. I knew it was hard for him. He was fighting a strong force, and he was slipping.

It was only a matter of time before the voice regained control, but we still gained something. We gained hope. If he was able to stay in control for as long as he did, he could eventually regain total control. Soon, the voice would be searching for a new victim to possess.

Within minutes afterwards, Alex dropped. Fighting the voice had drained all of his brain power and energy. It was similar to a child after having a seizure. He slept and slept. It wasn't until the next day when he finally woke up.

The next emotion was greed. This was both the least and the most annoying of his emotions. When he woke up, he raced over to his backpack and started going through it. It was like he was expecting something to have gone missing.

One-by-one, he pulled out the items and examined them. Once he had checked them all and made sure nothing had gone missing, he put everything back into his bag. Then, he held it in his arms and crawled over to my bag on his hands and knees.

Again, he emptied all of the contents and looked over them all. Then he did something unexpected. He kept a hold of it instead of giving it back to me. That was my first hint that it was greed. That day, we kept traveling, and again he led the way.

He didn't act as controlling as before, but he still had a look of confidence. However, this time it wasn't pure because he was paranoid. I had to take deep breaths. If I didn't, I would start screaming at him for dragging his feet so much.

When we finally took a break to eat, I wasn't allowed to eat anything. He turned his back to me and started shoveling food down his throat. I felt like I was babysitting a little kid. My stomach ached for food, but I didn't dare try to take any food from him. I was afraid of him getting mad at me again.

That time, convincing him to fight against the voice was even harder.

"Alex," I said, "you really need to stop listening to the voice. Don't you see what it's doing to you?"

"Never," he responded, "you only want me to stop listening to it because you're jealous that you do not hear it too."

"I promise that isn't the reason. Please just do this. If you do it once, I'll stop bothering you about it," I negotiated.

"Why should I listen to you, and what's so bad about the voice anyway?" he was trying and failing to mock me, "you know what? I think I'll keep listening to it just to spite you."

"Well, I guess you must really like sharing with the voice...," I trailed off.

"What do you mean?" he questioned, "I don't share with anyone."

"Well," I sighed dramatically for effect, "because the voice is inside of your head, you are sharing all of your thoughts with it. You probably didn't even think about it until now, did you?"

"No," he growled, "but I'm not going to share my thoughts with it anymore. Those are mine, and no one else can have any of them."

I watched as he focused on forcing the voice from his head. He started to sway back and forth. I thought he had freed himself from it, but then he started to stumble backwards. I watched as he crashed against the wall and fell to the ground.

I raced over to him, but he had been knocked unconscious. There was no blood, which was a good sign; but bruises were beginning to climb onto the surface of his skin. A slight bump began to rise from the back of his head.

On a normal day, I would have been nervous about him hitting his head so hard. That day, excitement took over my nerves. Alex was able to fight a lot longer than before. The first time he attempted to detach himself from the voice, he lost within a matter of seconds. This time he was persistent and he put up a good fight.

He also had a strong sense of urgency because the greed had been more powerful. This allowed him to last for at least fifteen minutes before he started to stumble and be taken over again.

I felt selfish. Food was the first thing that came to my mind. There wasn't anything I could do for him, and I reassured myself that it wasn't his fault. He wasn't the one that wouldn't let me eat, it was the voice.

The grip he had on the bags was as strong as gravity. I had to pry his fingers up one by one. I used both hands, but I still found myself struggling and having to pause and catch my breath.

When I finally freed one of the bags from his hands, I didn't bother searching through it to find water. I just dumped all of its contents out and desperately searched for water. I ripped off the cap and began to take huge gulps of water.

I felt my dry throat soaking it up like water in the desert. My next priority was food. I ate the first thing I could find without even looking to see what it was. I ate so quickly that I didn't even taste the food.

When I was full, I leaned my back against the wall and waited for Alex to wake back up. My eyelids began to feel heavier and heavier until they finally slipped down and I was forced into a deep sleep.

I didn't dream about anything, but that was exactly what I needed. I had to stop thinking so that I could just relax.

This went on for days. I would wake up, and Alex would have some sort of new emotion that was controlling him. Then, I would spend all day convincing him to try to fight the voice.

Each time, he was able to hold on for a little longer, but he still wasn't even close to reaching a breakthrough. After that, he would get knocked out and the process would repeat.

Although I wasn't the one battling, I felt like I was growing weaker every day. My flame of hope was growing smaller and smaller. It was barely burning, and soon I would be engulfed in darkness.

Fortunately, the emotions were all different levels of intensity, but each one found a different way to scare me. At one point, he felt guilty. No matter what I said, he wouldn't snap out of it. No matter how many heroic things I said he had done, he could back it up with a negative.

He told me stories about his life. There were so many things that he blamed himself for, yet he had nearly nothing to do with them. He couldn't have changed some of them. No matter what his reaction was, things would have ended up the same way.

The worst stories were those of death. With every person he had ever known to die, he could connect himself to their death and make it his fault. It pulled on my heartstrings, and I wanted to cry. It made me think of all the terrible things I had done and never given a second thought about.

I was finally able to convince him to fight the voice by telling him it would rid him of all of his guilt. I knew that I wasn't telling the entire truth, but I couldn't stand another minute of it. Afterwards I felt terrible.

The look of hope in his eyes was forever aflame. Getting rid of the guilt living inside him was like finding a strong flame in the dark; the type of flame that burned and never wavered, no matter how hard you tried to make it fade.

Sadness was just as bad. All he wanted to do was sit and cry about everything that had ever happened to him. The only thing that made it worse than the guilt was all of these things had happened. All the stories he told were true and terrible.

His childhood was miserably difficult. His parents acted as though they wanted nothing to do with him, and they treated him as a stranger. Things only got worse from there, especially when Ria died. After that, they completely checked out and they never said a word.

After he had fought and lost his battle, I sat against the wall with my head in my hands as I cried. I hated these feelings because I knew that I was the only one who could get rid of them.

My life had always been so easy. I didn't have to work for anything. I could ace tests without even thinking about them, and when I was in an awkward situation I always could find my way out of it and stay out of trouble.

I had everything at my fingertips, and now all of it was gone. The worst part was that I didn't even miss it. I was too confident that things could only make my life better. I thought that nothing could ever take a wrong turn.

When I woke up, Alex was sitting right next to me. His eyes were wide, and he looked like a little puppy who had been awaiting the arrival of its owner for days. He perked up instantly when I opened my eyes completely.

I wasn't exactly sure how, but I knew this emotion right away. It was puppy love. This was a weird kind of love in my opinion because it usually went one way. Yet, it was so strong that one person would do anything for the other, even if they weren't appreciated.

"Good morning. How'd you sleep? Are you hungry? Do you want me to get something for you to eat?" the words flew out of his mouth so fast I could barely make sense of them.

"I'm fine," was all that I answered. This was going to be a long day. I didn't know how to get him to leave me alone without being mean.

"Oh, well, okay then, tell me if you need anything. I'll be happy to assist you with whatever you need." His eyes were longing. He wanted to be wanted and feel important, but doesn't everyone?

"Thank you," I said sweetly. I hated leading him on like that, but I couldn't bring myself to be mean to his puppy eyes.

His smile was definitely worth the guilty feeling burying itself within me. I had felt so distant from him these past couple of days, and it was nice to be able to talk to him again. I also had felt unimportant for a really long time, and I would never want anyone else to feel that way.

I felt like I was back home where no one cared about anything that I did. They always seemed to care more about Annie, and I had always been jealous. She had more friends than I did, and they always seemed to last. My friendships were always short-lived.

My parents would always focus on her. I felt like they wished they hadn't had a second child sometimes. I knew it was mostly because I could take care of myself, and Annie wasn't ready to be on her own yet; but that didn't make me feel any less unwanted.

I was never encouraged. My family always ignored me when I talked to them about my accomplishments, and they were always getting excited over Annie's. Sometimes I wanted to disappear and never look back.

This maze had taken a lot of things from me, but finally I felt important. Even if it wasn't real, I wouldn't go back in time and keep it from happening.

While we were traveling, things seemed normal for the most part. The only difference was the look on Alex's face. The way he looked at me told me he would take a bullet for me. He would do anything for me, but that was exactly why I needed this emotion to leave him.

"Hey, Alex," I piped up.

"Yes," he sounded like an eager intern, itching to prove himself.

"I was wondering if you could do something for me..," I trailed off.

"Of course, what do you need?" he asked.

"You know that voice that's like in your head?" I questioned.

"I don't know what your talking about," he seemed disappointed.

"Are you sure that there isn't anything that's talking to you in your head and, umm giving you advice?" I wasn't exactly sure how to phrase it, so I did my best and hoped he would understand.

"Oh," he smiled, "are you talking about my conscience?"

"Yeah," my voice cracked a little bit. I had no idea how I was going to make him fight the voice if he thought it was his conscience.

"What about it?" he seemed curious now.

"I need you to fight against it, you know, try to get it to stop talking to you," I held my breath waiting for his response.

He opened his mouth, "Why would I want to do that?"

"I know that it sounds really weird, but I promise that I wouldn't ask you to do this if it wasn't super important," I bit my lip, and every second I waited, my jaw tightened. I tasted a faint trace of blood running along the edge of my mouth.

"If you think that it is important, I will. I promise that I will do this for you. I will fight against it, and I will win," he was confident that I only wanted what was best for him, and that was true. The only thing is that I didn't know what was going to happen to him if he won.

He took a few steps back from me and stood

perfectly balanced in an athletic stance. He linked his fingers together and held them against his stomach. His breathing was perfectly even, and I could see his stomach moving up and down as he breathed in and out.

He bent his head down, and the look on his face was pure determination. His eyes bulged out slightly, and I knew that he had started to fight against the voice. He didn't move a muscle, and I had a feeling that this time things were going to be different.

This time, he wasn't fighting for himself. He was fighting for me, and he didn't want to disappoint anyone. Almost everyone wanted to avoid letting down other people, and because he was being controlled by love, the strongest emotion, he had even more of a reason not to.

Even though this fight was mental, it was still nerve-racking. Then something unexpected happened. Gray-colored air started to come out of his mouth and nose. He appeared to be breathing out something, but I had no idea what it was.

It started to expand and replace all of the air in the area. I couldn't see anything. Everything smelled like rain, and the air felt damp. My first instinct was to run, but I had to push that away. I didn't know anything about this maze, and I could have run straight into a trap if I tried to escape.

Every once in a while, I would see sparks of light — but I wasn't sure if they were real or if my eyes were playing tricks on me. I stood and waited for something to happen. The anticipation was becoming too strong, and anything would be an improvement.

Then, I saw it. My eyes hadn't been playing tricks

on me. A rainbow was forming within the fog. I moved towards the light, and I wasn't surprised to find that it was wrapped around Alex. He was lying on the ground, and the palms of his hands were pressed against his face.

I knelt down next to him and placed my hand over his. A million explanations were passing through my head, and I had no idea what to believe or not. Alex could have failed to get rid of the voice, and maybe the fog and light was a coincidence. Maybe, he had beaten it and needed time to recover.

I didn't want to think about it, but there was always the possibility that he was dead. Through the fog I couldn't see if he was moving, but he had to be. I needed him to be alive.

CHAPTER XIV
ALEX

I never knew that so many colors existed. I had just fought the voice, and I had won the battle. Now I was lying on the ground, and I couldn't get up. Different colors kept flashing through my mind along with faces of people I had never even seen before.

Guilt bubbled up inside of me like a volcano about to explode. Erin had stayed with me through all of this, and I had treated her so badly. I ordered her around. I made her feel guilty. I filled her with depressing feelings. I made her uncomfortable. Worst of all, I had hit her.

It shouldn't have been the thing that stood out in my mind, but it was. I couldn't stop thinking about it. The thought stood in front of me like a lighthouse guiding a ship in the dark. I had struck her across the face with the back of my hand. It was something that no one should have ever even thought about. The memory wouldn't stop replaying itself in my head.

I felt sick to my stomach, and I couldn't stop thinking about what a monster I had become. All of it was because I had to listen to that stupid voice. I should have been better than that. Knowing who to trust shouldn't have been that hard. Choosing right should have been even easier. Yet, I still managed to mess that up.

My head felt like it was going to spin off. Opening my eyes seemed like the hardest thing in the world. It felt like there were a million layers I had to peel back one at a time. When I thought they were open, I still saw darkness— but there were shreds of light streaming through the black sheet in front of my face.

Then, I realized how stupid I was being. I still had my hands over my eyes. I lifted them from my eyes and felt the slight weight of them vanish. When I sat up, Erin was looking at me like I was her favorite person in the world.

"You have got to stop doing that!" she screamed at me. Her eyes were glistening with tears, and she wiped them off with the hem of her shirt.

"Doing what?" I still had no idea who I was these past few days.

"Making me think you're dead!" she acted as if it was an obvious question.

"Trust me," I told her, "it's better to worry that someone is dead than to be possessed and watch yourself turn into beast."

"YOU are not a beast," she said, "The VOICE is one, and it isn't your fault that it was stronger than you."

"Excuse me," I said sarcastically, "but I'm pretty sure that I'm stronger than a voice, or at least I should be..,"

"You're right," she rolled her eyes, "it must have just caught you off guard."

"Now that's a better explanation," I confirmed.

The rest of the day was awkward. I didn't know what I should say. There was a bruise in the shape of a hand on her face, and I knew it was from me. Her eyes were drooping from lack of sleep, and she looked pale.

I couldn't look at her without thinking, "What have I done?" I tried to avoid making eye contact when possible, but I didn't want her to think I was avoiding her. We never stopped for meal breaks, and I wondered how much ground we had lost in these past few days.

There was black fog hovering along the walls; but with every step, it grew thinner and thinner. However, it seemed to linger forever. The whole place smelled like wet dirt, and I hated the smell so much that I had to breathe through my mouth.

Our path gradually became narrower until Erin and I had to walk side-by-side. When I got a closer look at her, her expression was blank as usual. I desperately wanted to find something that would numb the pain of my guilt.

"I'm so sorry," I looked down at the ground. I was so ashamed that I couldn't hold it in any longer.

"What for? You know that you weren't the one who did any of that," she seemed confused.

"It's true that none of those things were my idea, but I still did all of them. Honestly, I could not feel more disappointed in myself. And I am so, so sorry. You should have left me to be eaten by cannibals. It's what I deserved," it felt good to finally let it out.

"I forgive you. That could have easily been me," I felt even worse because, she was being so nice about it. I wanted her to yell and scream at me. At least that way, I would feel like I was given some sort of punishment.

"But you weren't the one it happened to," I said flatly.

"What? Do you want me to be mad at you or something?" she exclaimed.

"I feel even worse because of how calm you are being about all of this. It makes me feel like a bad person. I don't know why, it just does," the look on my face was probably begging her to get angry, but she ignored it.

"You are not a bad person. You have never let me down, and we are a team. That means that when one of us falls, the other helps them up without any hesitation. We need to forgive each other; it is our only chance. We don't have anyone else," she cried.

"That's easy for you to say because you didn't hurt me. I did that to you," I gestured at her face. "That's the worst thing I've ever done, and you don't know how much I wish I could take it back."

"I am not trying to be mean but you can't take it back. You will never be able to take back what you did. All you can do is accept what has happened and just move on," she said sternly, and the conversation ended right as we reached a dead end.

There was a door looming in front of us. It was covered by long, silver panels that crossed over each other.

The handles were crystal balls, and rainbows reflected off of them. It was beautiful, but here looks were always deceiving.

I placed my hand on the knob, and I felt a shock go through me. I slowly twisted the knob, and the door slid open silently. In front of us was a white room. There were white walls, a white tile floor, and a white ceiling.

There was a long, glass table in front of us, and it was covered with goggles. The goggles were clear, and they were made out of a flexible plastic material. The tinted lenses looked black.

I grabbed two pairs off of the table and handed one of them to Erin. They were extremely lightweight, and the sides were sticky. When you pushed or pulled on the material you could mold it like silly putty.

I slid the goggles over my eyes, and the ends snaked out and attached together. There was a loud clicking noise, and they tightened around my face. I tried to pull them off, but they didn't budge.

I couldn't see anything through the dark lenses at first, but my eyes slowly adjusted. I was in a completely different place now. The white room that had once stood before me was now a lush, green meadow.

There were tall cherry trees, and the small pond was filled with clear, blue water and white swans. A slight breeze was blowing on my face — and when I closed my eyes, I could hear birds from far away.

The air tasted like citrus fruit, and it smelled like warm apple pie. I inhaled the savory aroma deeply before re-opening my eyes.

There was a long, wooden sign in front of me. It was similar to the ones that hung outside of family-owned bakeries and cafes, but this one was not an advertisement. To this day, I still don't know what to call it.

"THE PATH OF THE PAST" was carved into the dark wood, and the smaller letters below said "Reflection Road." I wouldn't have even noticed it if I hadn't been looking so closely. I started to walk towards it to get a closer look.

I was stuck in place while I was moving. No matter how long I walked, I never came any closer to the sign, and I was in the exact place I started in. I couldn't walk backwards or side-to- side, either. I was trapped in a single square foot.

I took an empty water bottle out of my backpack and threw it to see what would happen, but it never left my hand. It reached my fingertips, but then it slid back down into my hand.

I tried to throw something or run towards the sign over and over again, but it never worked. It felt like I was in a dream. None of the animals seemed to notice me, and they walked past me as if I didn't exist.

I wondered if I could change things again by closing my eyes. I squeezed my eyes shut and counted to twenty before I opened them again. Now, I wasn't even in the meadow anymore.

I was back home in the city. I had a bird's eye view, but I was still in my own body. It was like I was a ghost watching my own past. And and I were walking to the cemetery to visit Ria's grave. This was how we found Erin.

She was lying on the ground bleeding when we found her. If we had been any later, she could have died. I watched as we carried her home, and our parents came out of the shadows for the first time in ages.

I tried to get a closer look but I still couldn't change my position in any way. I had to stay where I was and observe from a distance. When I became bored, I closed my eyes. When I opened them, I was in the beginning of the maze.

And was in the middle of telling Erin and me about his first trip into the maze. I almost laughed when I saw the look on my face. Shock filled every inch of it. I couldn't believe my older brother had been hiding things from me.

Next, I was at the golden gate. This had been our first obstacle, but it still didn't fail to slice us apart. Our brains had to work inside out and backwards, and some of my worst scars were from that day. I wondered how long they would last.

Crossing the bridges was our next obstacle. In all, there had been four of them. The broken bridge, what I liked to call bleeding bridge, the ice bridge, and the fire bridge. This tested our knowledge even further — and once we passed this obstacle, there was no possible way for us to go back. The bridges had been destroyed, and we could only go forward.

Then, we faced "leaps of faith." These ranged from zip lines, to free falls, to monkey bars. They were probably one of my least favorite things to pass because falling to your death didn't seem like a pleasant way to go.

Although the Creature Chambers were terrifying,

they were probably one of the simpler things to pass. Most of the time, we just had to use common sense. There weren't any puzzles or riddles we had to figure out. Yes, we did have to battle dangerous crossbreeds and we almost died, but the only permanent damage we were left with was a missing shoe...

The water was one of the few obstacles that were fun, but it was terrifying at the same time. We got to ride dolphins (which was pretty awesome), but the serpents took away most of the fun. The whirlpools intrigued me, but I didn't want to spend any more time around them than I had to.

Then, there were the tangled webs. They were scary, and the pain from them was by far the worst and most permanent. My whole body still ached from losing my older brother, and the memory would always be lingering within my mind. I don't think I will ever leave this memory behind because part of me doesn't want to.

I needed to remember And as the brave person he was. As much as it hurt me, I had to remember that in a way, it was his choice to die. He was doing the right thing. I'm proud to call him my brother.

Afterwards, we went to the diamond mine. At the time I thought that it was stupid to go, but it ended up being one of our smartest decisions. We couldn't have asked for a better opportunity to collect valuable information.

We learned about the portals, something we had only dreamed of before; and we learned how to use them. Behind some of the portals, a world filled with evil existed. This world was distant, but it was slowly drifting into our world. I craved more facts on this topic.

The stars we saw after leaving the mine were beautiful. I had never seen anything like them before, and I wish we could have stayed there longer. However, the peace was destroyed when a cannibal fight erupted. We also saw our first dark portal.

Next thing I knew, we were blindly running and going through portals to escape a cannibal who was chasing us. Erin and I didn't even have to communicate with each other. We both followed our instincts, and fortunately they told us the same things.

What happened next was a blur. We were in a room, and we had finally escaped — or at least I think we escaped; but then the room was filled with some sort of gas. When you smelled it, it filled you with a soothing feeling. I ended up unconscious.

When I returned to reality, I was in a different room. I didn't recognize it at all, but I did recognize one thing. The things surrounding Erin and I were cannibals. Their crazed eyes were the first thing that I saw, and they burned through my soul. I would be dead right now if Erin hadn't risked her life to save me.

When we almost starved to death, I owed Erin everything for saving me. I decided to experiment by eating a vine to pay off my debt. She had purposely cut herself and given me her blood after the cannibals nearly drained me of my life, so eating a vine was the least I could do.

I still don't know what happened after I ate the vine. It could have been real or simply just a dream.

Anyway, I thought that I was in the land of the dead. I was in a new body, the body of a ghost.

I saw how everything would turn out if I didn't return. Everyone was happy, but what shocked me the most was possibly seeing Kate. She was the girl And watched die in the maze years ago. Cannibals attacked her, and she couldn't be saved.

She told me there was someone watching over me, and I should listen to their voice when I heard it. Then, I was whisked away to a room that made me feel like I was on trial for murder.

The people there told me I was special — and for the first time ever, they were going to save someone from dying. Shortly after, I "woke up" in my own body again. I was confused, and I didn't know what to believe. I still don't, but I have gotten used to being in the dark.

Then, something presented its self. Something so horrific that I couldn't even imagine it in my wildest nightmares. It may have only been a voice, but it had the power to possess me. It controlled me, and I willingly let it. While I was possessed, I was a monster. I knew I would never stop feeling ashamed of the way I acted.

I treated Erin like she was a slave to me, but she stayed by my side. I confessed everything I had ever done or thought about doing. I was greedy, and I nearly caused Erin to starve to death because I didn't want to share anything with anyone. She didn't even try to fight me because she was too afraid.

My brain was on overload. It felt like I was looking into a double mirror. The same images appeared over and over again, and there was no ending. It was an endless cycle, and I couldn't break free from it. I felt like I was left to watch my life on replay for forever.

Finally, I realized why I had to watch things over and over again. In all of the memories, there was one thing that just didn't make sense. Each time I saw it, it became even more obvious. There was a face in all of the pictures, and it was watching our every move.

It was the face of a woman. Sometimes she appeared to be old, and other times she seemed to be young. She was always in black and white, and her dark hair was loosely pinned behind her head. Her eyes were black holes, and her pupils were bright white.

Her face seemed to go in a cycle of young to old. The first time I noticed her she looked like she was barely into her twenties, but she gradually aged. Her expressions became more tired, and her skin became more wrinkled.

When she looked fully aged, the process would reverse. Her face would tighten, her eyes would brighten, and it seemed like the fire of hope within her became stronger.

Her face became closer every time I saw it, and I was able to have a clearer vision of what she really looked like. Then, I heard her speak. I knew the voice instantly. It was the voice that had been controlling me. I immediately broke free from whatever this was, and I pulled my goggles away from my face.

I felt sweat running down my face, and my throat was dry. I was starting to panic. I had gotten scared and started to freak out many times before, but this time was different. I was shaking, scared, and stupid. I had no idea what was going on.

I tried to tug the goggles off of Erin's face; but she held onto them and pushed me away. This maze was like a drug. It made you want more and more. Whatever it did, you craved it. And you could never get enough.

It's a good thing that I was stronger than Erin. I had to tear the goggles from her face, and when I finally did, she looked furious. I knew she would be mad at me, and I hoped I hadn't just screwed something up.

"What was that for?" she screamed in my face.

"I saw how that movie ends, and I don't think it's something you'd want to see. Trust me," I had expected this reaction, but I hadn't thought of what my response would be.

"Well then," she scoffed, "if you are such an expert, why don't you tell me about how it ends. I lost my opportunity to figure it out on my own."

"The voice," I whispered so quietly that I could barely hear the words as they left my mouth.

"What did you just say?" she started to look worried now instead of angry.

"I saw the voice's face. I had to look closely, but she's in all of my memories. My brain had just chosen to ignore it," I explained.

"I'm so sorry," her eyes were wide, like she was about to cry.

"Don't be. If we were watching the same memories, then you should feel like a hero. You have nothing to be sorry for, and everything you've done has been helpful," I argued.

"If I had never come into your life, then you would have dodged a bullet. I don't think you realize how much pain and loss I've caused you," she replied.

"You're exactly what And and I needed to have in our lives. And learned to love again. Without you, he would have spent his whole life shutting out other people and hiding in the dark. I finally have a family again, and this adventure has been priceless," I responded.

"Ugh," she sighed. Her head was tilted down and she acted like it was nothing, but I knew she was just avoiding eye contact.

She thought all of this was her fault. In a way, I guess it was her fault — but everyone who got hurt chose to take the risk. I wanted her to know that we knew what we were up against when we agreed to help her, but she was burnt out and didn't feel like arguing anymore.

"What, what did she look like?" she stuttered.

I explained the complicated image as well as I could. I told her about seeing the face and how it was hanging in front of my face; but my mouth wouldn't allow me to explain everything I wanted to.

The rest of the day, I felt like I was being followed. I saw the voice's face everywhere, but I wasn't sure if it was real or my imagination. Sometimes, I wondered if my whole life was a dream I hadn't woken up from yet.

Maybe I lived in another world and none of this was real. Maybe I was still sitting at home with And and my imagination was going wild. A volcano of thoughts erupted in my head, and they surrounded my brain.

Night was cold, and we had to build a fire. I couldn't get close enough to it, and I felt flames licking at the edges of my skin. My skin felt like a sheet of ice, and I couldn't feel my fingertips or the ground below me.

"I saw home," Erin murmured, "but I don't want to go back."

"Why not?" for a moment, my mind was distracted from the temperature outside.

"I saw the future, or at least I think it was the future," she admitted.

"What happened?" I asked.

"Ann-Annie was dead. She didn't even end up in the maze. She died on the island from an escaping prisoner. I wasn't there for anything. I was gone when they said goodbye, I was gone when they prayed for her, and I was gone when they let her go," she shivered.

"It's hard to tell what's real and what isn't anymore. Your sister is probably fine; we just have to find her," I reminded her. I pulled her closer to me and leaned towards the fire.

Her lips were tinted with purple, and her teeth were chattering. Her face glowed orange from the fire, and the space in front of us was blurry from the smoke. It smelled like an old campfire that had been burning for days on end.

I didn't even remember falling asleep, but when I woke up my skin was covered in blisters. The edges of my clothes had been singed, and my hands were covered in ash. The fire was a thin, steady, vicious flame of death. I was grateful for my lack of skill when it came to building fires. If it had been any bigger, I could have been burned to death.

I started to brush the ash from my skin. At first, flakes of skin came off with it; but then strips of skin began to peel off. I didn't have first aid training like And had, so I only knew the basics. This was much, much different.

When I looked to the side, I saw that Erin had been affected by the fire as well. The burns on her skin were far more severe than mine, but drops of blood had stained some of her skin. Her face had luckily been shielded, but her hands and arms were a disaster.

At first I thought she was alright. After all, her face had been protected. But then I tried to wake her up. That's when I realized her skin was cold to the touch, and her body was limp. I tried to wake her up over and over, but nothing was working.

The circumstances drove me to do something completely insane. I had never considered doing this before, but now I had to. I was going to ask the voice for help. I wasn't quite sure how to summon it, but when I turned off the security in my mind it came to me.

"I see you've finally realized how much you need me," it spoke inside of my head.

"I don't need to sit here and listen to you praise yourself, I want you to heal Erin and me," I tried to keep things short, sweet, and to the point.

"I won't help you if you don't appreciate me. I am not your servant. Do not disrespect me," it warned.

"I'm sorry," my apology was fake but hopefully it couldn't tell, "Will you please help me?"

"Yes," it responded, "but I want something in

return."

"What do you want?" I groaned.

"It isn't very difficult. I only want to test your loyalty, and I want to see what lengths you would go to for the ones you love."

"What is it?" I felt my face tighten. I probably looked like a crazed murderer who wanted nothing more than to kill someone.

"I want you to sacrifice your left hand," it took me a while to filter the request because it seemed like a joke.

"You want what?" I exclaimed.

"You must use the blade of sacrifice to cut off your hand. Only then will I help you," it demanded.

"Is there any other way I can gain your help?" I begged.

"No," it said firmly, "and if I were you, I would start soon. The blisters on your skin are becoming more permanent as we speak, and your companion is in a coma. That is why she hasn't woken yet, and she might not if you don't move quickly."

"I'll do it," I agreed. I couldn't imagine watching Erin die and being left alone.

"Just to clarify things," it explained, "I will heal you, and once your hand is gone I will heal her."

"How do I know that you'll actually help her?" I questioned.

"You'll just have to trust me — and if you're going to ask me to heal her first, the answer is no. I need to make sure you are going to follow through," it seemed like she had read my mind.

"Did you just read my mind?" I was furious.

"No, but the expression on your face tells your every thought. By the way, when I say every, I truly mean it..," the voice trailed off, and then it was gone.

An arched blade appeared at my feet, and I knew what I had to do. When I picked it up, the pain immediately vanished from my body. There was no trace of injury left anywhere. I ran my fingers along the metal handle and the top of the sleek, gray blade.

I barely felt the blade slash through my flesh and bone. All I felt was a cold, crisp, tingling feeling. It was easier than I had imagined it. I felt like I was cutting through melting butter. The cut healed almost as quickly as it was made; but to my disappointment, my hand was gone forever. It vanished into midair, and the only thing remaining was a thin, crooked scar.

CHAPTER XV
ERIN

What had just happened was a mystery. I fell asleep near the fire, and I felt the flames dancing across my skin. I shielded my face as best as I could. I was certain that it had been real. I couldn't move because I didn't have the strength to reposition myself.

Now, I had woken up from what seemed like a terrible nightmare. What I saw was even worse. Alex was standing with a long, curved blade in his hand. The blade was covered in odd symbols, and his other hand was missing.

"Oh, my God!" I screamed, "What is going on? Are you suicidal?"

"Hardly," he responded. I could see him picking apart his brain for some sort of logical explanation, but none was coming to mind.

"Answer me," I pleaded. I needed to know what

was happening.

"I had to do this," he cried, "There-there was no other way."

"I have no idea what you're talking about," I prayed for some sort of story that would tie all of this madness together. Even a completely insane explanation would be better than nothing because at that moment, I wanted to cry from the confusion that was overwhelming me.

"The voice threatened to kill me unless I sacrificed my hand, and it doesn't bargain. It was deal or death; I chose deal. If I was actually suicidal, do you really think that my hand would be healed after what I just did?" he rambled. There was something wrong with this picture, but I couldn't put my finger on it.

"I suppose," I sighed, "but why didn't you wake me up? We could have talked about this; but instead, you went crazy and cut off your hand." Why wasn't he being reasonable?

"Desperate times call for desperate measures," he was trying to sound calm, cool, and confident, but he wasn't going to fool me. This discussion may have come to an end, but I planned to return to it soon.

As usual, we took random twists and turns as we walked through the maze. We had abandoned our left turn strategy after we passed the broken bridges. There was no point in continuing it after that because there was no longer a way for us to return to Millennia. All we could do was hope we chose turns that would lead us in the right direction.

The entire time, Alex was running his fingers along

where his hand used to be. He looked so sad, and I was worried that he was going to explode with tears; but he kept his head held high, and he took long, deep breaths. I felt sorry for him, but he was starting to make me angry. I wanted him to give me more information about what had happened.

Then, something unexpected happened. We weren't in a maze anymore. We were walking along a path. It was almost like we had wandered into a whole other world. At first, I thought I was in a dream; but as hard as I tried, I couldn't wake up.

In the distance, I could see a tall mountain looming overhead. It looked like the type of thing you would see during a chase scene in an action movie. The first thought that crossed my mind was, "Damn it, I bet we'll have to climb that wall of death." If we did have to climb it, things would be interesting to say the least.

We were walking on top of rust-colored powder, and it made it almost impossible to move. Whenever I lifted up my foot, a ton of powder would come with it. I felt like I was dragging my feet through a pool of concrete.

The sun was blazing, and it nearly blinded me when I looked up. However, the heat seemed to bounce right off of me. I didn't break a sweat the entire time. We had to walk uphill, and the straps of my backpack kept loosening themselves; I was constantly readjusting them and having to push my backpack higher up on my back.

Gusts of wind sent powder flying everywhere. It covered every visible surface, and it was impossible to brush off my skin. I could feel it in my mouth, and I heard a crunching noise when I moved my jaw.

This went on for three days. We hiked towards the mountain without talking or taking our eyes off of it. I wasn't even sure if we were supposed to be going there, but it seemed like the only shot we had.

We came across a few miniature streams, and I tried to wash the powder out of my mouth. However, the water was a liquid version of the powder, and it only made things worse. The taste that was left in my mouth was dirt and chalk.

The nights were still cold, but Alex was very cautious about the fire. He barely kept the flame alive, and it usually died within minutes. He wouldn't let it burn once we started to fall asleep, so this made the nights long and miserable.

We ended up having to become nocturnal to avoid freezing to death while we slept. This made things bearable, but we didn't cover as much ground because we had to stop and build fires every hour to warm back up.

We also couldn't see as well in the dark, so we didn't know where we were going most of the time. I'm not sure if it was just me, but I felt like I was constantly tripping over things and missing steps when the ground level changed.

"Why are we doing this?" I asked.

"Doing what?" he responded.

"You know what I mean," I narrowed my eyes, "we have barely talked to each other for days, and now you have come up with this weird nocturnal schedule. I want to know why, and you are going to tell me." I raised my eyebrows while I was waiting for a response.

"Just to clarify, I don't have to if I don't want to. But if it means that much to you, then I will tell you," he stated.

"So?" my eyes were wide, and they were glaring right at him.

"I lied when I said that the voice threatened to kill me," he looked away, "I screwed up when I was building the fire. It spread while we were sleeping, and I was badly burned. I was freaking out, and I didn't know what to do. So, I summoned the voice. We made deal, and I sacrificed my hand for my health." Tears were forming in his eyes, and he was trying his hardest to blink them away.

"By any chance, was I a part of this deal?" I bit my lip, and my stomach tightened while I waited for the answer.

"No," he blurted too quickly, "I never would have made a decision that involved you if you weren't there. I didn't tell you about it because if I'd asked you for advice, it wouldn't have helped me," he was stuttering, and words were flying out of his mouth before they could even reach his brain.

"Are you hiding something from me? Was I hurt, and did you do this for me?" When the response didn't come right away, I knew what it was going to be. It made me feel sick to my stomach; but then he looked me straight in the eye.

"You were perfectly fine. The only damage was the burnt edges of your clothing. I did this for myself. Not everything is about you," he sounded frustrated.

I still didn't know why, but that surprised me. I knew no one was perfect, but it seemed like Alex was. He had never done anything selfish before that. However, his face stayed completely serious, and his hands were planted at his sides. I knew that he wasn't lying.

"Okay," I was in a daze, but I still needed to face reality. All people thought of themselves — and ultimately, they would always make sure they stayed alive, no matter what the consequences were. He wasn't being selfish, he was just being human. It just went to prove, no length of time would be enough to find someone who was truly perfect.

Normally, I wouldn't have thought his actions were selfish; but he knew as well as I did that he needed his hand for this mission. There was always a second solution to a problem, and he should have let me be a part of this decision. It affected me almost as much as it affected him. Plus, I might have been able to find a loophole that he had missed.

We started to turn our schedule back to normal when the weather began to heat up. I still wasn't sure how the weather could change underground; but I was grateful for it, even if I didn't understand it.

Late into the next night, we finally reached the mountain. It was nothing like I expected it to be. From far away, it looked like we could climb it in a matter of hours; but this mountain was immense, and it could take days to get to the top.

It stretched along the horizon forever, and I couldn't see where it began or where it ended. There weren't any small gaps or holes that could be crawled through. It was like a giant rock-climbing wall without the safety ropes or tacky-colored rocks.

There were handholds and places for your feet spread throughout the surface, but none of the faces were tilted in our favor. We could either go straight up, or we could go backwards and be upside down for part of the time.

The obvious choice was to go straight up. I wasn't in the mood for taking a risk, and sticking to logic seemed like a good idea this time. I looked up, but the top of the mountain was nowhere in sight. All I could see was a small ledge about a quarter mile up.

It was only big enough to hold one person, and we weren't sure how sturdy it would be. So, we decided that I would climb up to the ledge in the morning. From there, Alex and I would use the ropes to get him and his stuff up to the ledge.

We planned to keep doing this each day. We had to make sure we were never on the same ledge. We didn't know how sturdy they were, and we didn't want them to come crumbling down. Plummeting to my death or near death wasn't something I wanted to face. Hopefully there would be enough ledges for our plan to work.

When I woke up the next morning, the sun was beating down, and beads of sweat formed on my forehead. I imagined my face as red as a lobster and my skin sizzling in the intense heat.

I removed everything I wasn't going to need from my backpack. All that remained was a day's supply of food and water and the rope for getting Alex and the rest of our supplies onto the ledge.

The rock practically disintegrated when I touched it. Whenever I held onto a piece for too long, it would break off or crumble in my hands. I would have to desperately grab a new handhold. I had planned a route that looked easy, but I no longer thought it was going to be a possibility. I was practically on the opposite side from where I wanted to be.

There was a small crack that went straight up the mountain, and it was just big enough for me to jam my hands and feet into. I slipped into it and pulled myself up. The skin on my hands was cracking, and I could feel the back of my neck starting to peel from being sunburned.

Soon enough, it began to rain. Water filled the crack that was holding me up, and it started to push me back down. Yes, I had been hoping for something to cool me off, but this was definitely not what I'd had in mind.

I thought about dropping and falling to the ground. I could always try again tomorrow, or maybe we could find another way; but when I looked down, I realized I'd climbed further than I thought. The ground was a million miles away. Thinking about the pain I would feel after smashing my face into the powdery ground made me cringe.

I turned my head towards the ledge. It seemed like I could reach out my hand and touch it. I only needed to make it a little bit further, and then I would finally be able to rest. I wanted to be excited, but that feeling needed to stay on hold for now. I still had to get there, and when I did, I didn't know if it would be strong enough to support me.

When my palms finally pressed against the ledge, I felt pride surge within me. I had finally been able to accomplish something difficult on my own. No one had to stop what they were doing and come to my rescue, and no one had to guide me through what to do.

There was a small gap between the ledge and the side of the mountain. I pulled out one of the ropes and wedged it into the gap. Then, I tied it around my waist. It most likely wouldn't hold me if I fell off of the ledge, but it would give me a brief moment to catch myself before I fell. It felt like a security blanket — it didn't necessarily keep me safe, but it comforted me.

I was exhausted, and I fell into the arms of sleep as soon as my head touched the ledge's surface. All night I had nightmares about falling. I kept waking up after dying in my dream, and when I opened my eyes, I was as far from the edge as possible.

When the sun rose, I sat on the edge of the ledge with my feet dangling below me.

When Alex woke up, I tied the ropes together and lowered them towards him. As expected, we didn't have enough rope to reach him. This meant he would have to go about twenty feet on his own before reaching it.

He was surprisingly quick for someone with one hand. He looked like a dancer gliding up the side of the mountain. His hand was never in the same place for more than a few seconds, and he made smart decisions quickly.

By the time he reached the rope, I didn't think he

would even need it anymore. He tied it around his waist; but luckily, he never ended up needing it. If he did, I wasn't quite sure what I was going to do. By the time he reached the ledge, I was scrambling to get off of it so he could get on.

"I guess having one more hand than me isn't going to help you beat me," he cocked his head.

"Just so you know, if we weren't on the side of a mountain right now, I would have just slapped you in the face," I widened my eyes and shrugged.

"I know you wouldn't do that. You wouldn't hurt a fly," he grinned.

"Wanna bet?" I gave him false dagger-eyes.

"What's on the table," he mocked me. I wanted to crack a smile; but my eyes were locked, and I wasn't going to let go. This had become a contest, and I wasn't about to lose. He tried to say a few more clever things to make me break, but he was unsuccessful.

"Alright!" he finally accepted defeat, "you win! Now please just stop giving me that look because it's really starting to creep me out."

"It's good to know I'm still winning all of the arguments because your one hand isn't stopping you from beating me at everything else," I laughed, but I still felt embarrassed for losing to someone who only had one hand.

Alex swung his leg over the ledge, and he used his hand to pull the rest of his body onto the ledge. He rolled onto his back and looked up at me. I was clinging to the side of the mountain, and my feet were crammed into a deep crack. There weren't any handholds, so I leaned into the opening as much as I could.

"You better get climbing if you want to reach the next ledge before night," he gestured up with his hand. The next ledge was an even further climb than the first one was, and it looked far less stable. I needed to get there as quickly as possible. I didn't know if it could hold me; and if it was weak, I would have to keep climbing until I found a new ledge.

I kept my feet and hands in the crack as I moved upwards. Climbing like this slowed me down, but at least I was safe. I went along like this for a while, and the crack became narrower and narrower as I went. Soon, I couldn't even fit my hands in it. The handholds nearby were too small for me to use, so I had to backtrack. The handholds below me were slightly wider, and I could hold onto them with my fingertips.

I snaked back and forth looking for the best handholds as I moved upwards. Even then, I still had to move quickly. Bits of rock would disintegrate when I moved my hands; and when I pushed myself upward, the ledges supporting my feet broke off and disappeared.

I climbed slightly past the ledge and prepared for it to break when I stepped onto it. My hands were still gripping the nearest handholds, and I was slowly lowering my feet onto the ledge. It didn't break when I put most of my weight onto it, but I still didn't trust it.

I waited for a while before letting go of my handholds and relying on the ledge to support me. My muscles felt tired from holding myself up for such a long time. Then, I realized the ledge hadn't been supporting me, the handholds were. The ledge was weak, and it almost immediately collapsed. I didn't have time to grab the handholds above me, and I started to fall.

I watched the ground come closer and closer to me. Piles of rocks lined the mountain, so I knew I had no chance of surviving the impact. I was clawing at the side of the mountain, but every handhold I caught broke as soon as my fingers wrapped around it.

Finally, I found a small space where there was a rock missing. I flung my hand towards it, and slid my fist into the small space. There was nowhere for me to put my other hand or my feet. I pressed down on my fist with my other hand, and tried to push myself upward. All the energy in my body had been drained, so I barely moved.

Blood was spilling out of my hand and sticking to my skin. I tried to ignore it, but my hand was starting to slip. My whole body was shaking, and my ears were ringing. I looked down to see where the ledge I'd been on landed, and luckily it had gone straight down. The ledge Alex was on wasn't affected, but I couldn't see him anywhere.

I froze. Where was he? Was he alright? Had he been knocked down by the other ledge and fallen? My body felt numb. All I could think about was Alex. If he died, it would be my fault. I didn't think I could stand the sight of another dead body, especially his.

"Erin, you need to calm down," I heard his voice in my head, and all I could think was, "great, now I'm hearing the voice of someone who might be dead." However, the sound of his voice still calmed me down and made me relax.

I stopped struggling, and I focused on my breathing. The little voice in my head was counting the number of breaths I had taken, and somewhere along the way my mind made a decision. When I reached my fiftieth breath, I was going to drop or try to move upward.

My eyes were closed, and I was squeezing them together as tightly as I could. I saw colored dots everywhere when I finally opened my eyes. I knew I wouldn't be able to let go, so my only option was to go up.

When I looked up, I thought my mind was playing tricks on me. I saw Alex sitting in a large gap inside of the mountain. It looked like a cave, and I wondered how I had missed it before. It was turned away from me, so I couldn't have seen it when I fell (unless I was looking for it); but I should have noticed it on my way up.

"Are you finally going to stop waiting for your death?" Alex teased.

"What's your problem?" I was starting to get defensive, "Why did you just let me sit here thinking you were dead? I was going to die any second!"

"I tried to talk to you, but I didn't want to frighten you. Getting you up here is going to be hard enough, so I didn't want to make it any harder. Also, you were only there for about five minutes. I wouldn't have let you sit there for hours," he seemed sincere, but at the same time he was annoyed. He thought it was stupid for me to be arguing with him instead of climbing towards the cave.

"Fine," I mumbled, "can you toss me a rope so I can get up? There aren't any handholds around here," I gestured to the area around me with my free hand.

"Well, that was easy," he seemed surprised.

"What are you talking about?" I demanded.

"I was expecting you to be difficult and not want help from anyone else," he answered, "I did not think you would willingly accept help from me, and I never thought you would ask for it."

"Well, you can't blame me. Most people act differently when they're one wrong move away from plummeting to their death," I spat.

"Now that's the Erin that I was expecting," he laughed to himself as he lowered a rope down to me. I wrapped it around my free hand a few times, and then I tugged on it twice. I was hoping Alex would get the hint to start pulling me up, and fortunately he did.

When I reached Alex, I realized he actually was sitting in a cave. When he had his feet over the side, I was expecting it to be a small hallowed out area. This was a massive room. It was tall enough to stand up, and it was so long that I couldn't see the end.

As I expected, there were no lights. This meant we would have to be as quiet as possible. We didn't want to draw attention from anything living it the shadows that wanted to kill us. The air was cool; and compared to the scorching sun, I felt like I was in an igloo.

"How did you find this place?" I asked in awe.

"Well, when you decided to break that last ledge," he smirked, "I had to come to your rescue, and that's when I found it. There was a sheet over it that looks just like the mountain. I tried to grab onto one of the handholds painted on it, and I ended up pulling down the whole thing. Luckily, I did not fall and I ended up here." His voice was overly dramatic, and it seemed like he had rehearsed this moment a million times in his head.

"Have you looked around at all?" I wondered.

"Not really," his eyes scanned across the room, "I decided to wait until you were safe, and I wanted to wait for you. I knew I would never hear the end of it if I had started looking around without you."

"You know me way too well; let's start checking this place out," I wanted to get as far away from the entrance as possible, "maybe we can find another way to get to the top. Then we won't have to worry about falling. It would probably be way more efficient, too." I was talking too fast, and I really needed to shut my mouth. I couldn't let Alex know I was scared to go back out.

"Not so fast," he warned, "we need to be prepared for what might happen. We have no idea what is ahead of us, and if we start coming across dead ends, we need to turn back. Climbing the mountain will be faster than having to navigate another maze."

"Exactly," I choked down disappointment. I was hoping that he would be all over finding another way, but he just had to be the smart one here. We had climbed a decent portion of the mountain, and in another week we could be at the top. Time was our worst enemy, and whether or not we beat it was up to us.

As I had guessed, we were crawling on our hands and knees. It wasn't as practical as walking, but we needed to be as stable as possible. When we were closer to the ground, it was easier for us to feel around with our hands. It was less likely for us to run into anything, and we eliminated the possibility of tripping.

I felt like a blind person. I had to rely on my hands to know where I was going, and I couldn't see anything behind me or in front of me. I had a rope tied around my ankle, and it was attached to Alex's wrist. I went first because I was smaller; if we ended up in a small space, it would be easier for me to turn around than Alex.

I could tell we were moving upward, but the slope was almost nonexistent. I waved my hand around in front of me because I didn't want to run into anything. When we came across a turn, my hand would smack into the wall in front of me. We were going through so many twists and turns, I felt like we might be going around in circles.

Finally, we came to another room. This one was circular in shape, but it had the same tarp-like sheet covering the entrance. We pulled it down and looked down to see how much progress we had made.

The last cave area was much farther down than I thought it would be. The incline we were traveling at must have been much steeper than it felt. A smile spread across my face because this way of traveling was faster than climbing up the side of the mountain.

We folded up the tarp so we could keep track of our progress when we looked back down at the mountain. It was starting to get dark outside. Alex didn't want to be wandering in total darkness, and we couldn't risk having to stop before we reached the next room; so we decided to stay here for the night and continue on in the morning.

I used the tarp as a pillow; and although it wasn't much softer than the ground, it made me feel more comfortable. The familiarity of having my head slightly inclined allowed me to go right to sleep; and when I woke up, I felt fully refreshed and ready to travel.

We were able to get through three different rooms that day. It still didn't seem like we were making very much progress while climbing; but at the end of the day, we were almost halfway up the mountain. There weren't any more ledges on the side of the mountain, so it was a good thing we found another way to scale the mountain.

The tunnels were starting to become narrower. Every day, we had to crouch a little further to fit through them. The rooms were also becoming further and further apart. We had to move quickly if we wanted to get from one to the next before dark.

By the time we reached the final stretch, we had to slide along on our stomachs. My shirt was torn up, and my skin was covered in scrapes. The last room was much, much smaller than the others had been, and I felt like I would fall out of it if I moved while I was sleeping.

There weren't any tunnels after this room, so we had to climb along the face of the mountain again. My newly-developed fear of heights didn't make me a fan of this, but the climb looked short enough to complete in a few hours — that is if everything went smoothly.

The handholds all looked decently sized, and they were all fairly close together. I tried to keep my breathing as steady as possible, and I focused on it to keep my mind from drifting. Thoughts of falling ran through my mind, and they were difficult to push away.

When I finally reached the top of the mountain, I wanted to scream with victory. Alex wasn't far behind me. When he reached the top, we both looked at each other. For once, we both knew what the other was thinking: "We did it."

The top of the mountain was long and flat. The surface was wide, so I wasn't worried about falling off. Even with the sun streaming through the clouds overhead, the air was frigid and I started to shiver.

From here, I could see everything. The walls of the maze looked scattered, and I could see where all of the different obstacles were. I felt like I was on top of the world. Looking ahead, I could see how much further we had to travel. We had covered an amazing amount of ground, but the maze extended further than I ever could have imagined.

I wanted to look at everything, but my eyes kept getting drawn back to one particular spot. There was a large gap in the center of the maze. There were no walls around it, and in the center of it was an immense building.

The building looked like a grand palace, and it was built with the same materials as a castle. The walls were covered in stone, and there were brick arches spread throughout. Although it was beautiful, beauty isn't what drew me to it.

Surrounding the palace was a wall of fire. The flames were steady, and they never wavered. There was no burnt land below it, and no steam overhead. It looked so real, but it had to be some sort of illusion. I couldn't stop staring at it, but I couldn't think of anything else it could be. My mind was spinning, and it was impossible for me to make sense of things; but I did know one thing for sure — whatever it was, it scared me to death.

"What is that thing over there?" I was hoping Alex would know some sort of story or legend about the mysterious building.

"I have no idea," he confessed, "but that's a question that I would like to find the answer to."

"Well, I'm thinking that I know where our next destination is," I smirked.

"I think you are right," he answered.

ABOUT THE AUTHOR

Abigail Price is from Northern Nevada where she is currently a high school student. Through the Reflection is the first book she has written, and today Abigail continues to write while also perusing her education, athletics, and volunteer work.